Zero Gravity

Zero Gravity

SHARON ENGLISH

The Porcupine's Quill

Library and Archives Canada Cataloguing in Publication

English, Sharon, 1965–
   Zero gravity / Sharon English.

ISBN-13: 978-0-88984-279-3
ISBN-10: 0-88984-279-5

   I. Title.

PS8559.N5254Z47 2006   C813'.6   C2006-904444-9

Copyright © Sharon English, 2006.

1   2   3   4   •   08   07   06

Published by The Porcupine's Quill, 68 Main St, Erin, Ontario NOB 1TO.
http://www.sentex.net/~pql

Readied for the press by John Metcalf.
Copy edited by Doris Cowan.

Represented in Canada by the Literary Press Group.
Trade orders are available from University of Toronto Press.

We acknowledge the support of the Ontario Arts Council and the Canada Council for the Arts for our publishing program. The financial support of the Government of Canada through the Book Publishing Industry Development Program is also gratefully acknowledged. Thanks, also, to the Government of Ontario through the Ontario Media Development Corporation's OMDC Book Fund.

Canada Council
for the Arts

Conseil des Arts
du Canada

Canadä

ONTARIO ARTS COUNCIL
CONSEIL DES ARTS DE L'ONTARIO

Contents

Heartfelt thanks especially to Greg Hollingshead, John Metcalf, J. D. Pipher and my parents for their significant contributions to this book.

The Cosmic Elfs

I grew up in small-town Ontario, moved away for university, moved to Toronto to start working, but after four years the work-station walls were closing in and I was spending part of day in the washroom reading children's books. Then I had a panic attack.

I was sitting in a stall with *Peter Pan* on my knees when a co-worker opened the washroom door and called my name. Apparently I was wanted. I arrived at my boss's office to find her seated at the conference table with our VPDP, or vice president of development and production: a twitchy, beige-suited man whom I'd spoken to only once, during a quiet elevator ride in which he'd turned and, as if clearing the air between us, said, 'You're anorexic, aren't you?' Just slim, I'd assured him. 'Well, it's everywhere,' he said with a grunt, and made a shooing gesture at our reflections in the elevator's brassy wall. Now in front of my boss and him lay a document, which for a giddy moment caused me to fear that sinister conclusions had been drawn about my washroom habits. But it was actually a report I'd recently submitted, called 'The Proposed Implementation of MDIC Evaluations in HR Restructuring: An Assessment', a creation I'd been able to produce only by writing at home with a glass of brandy and Metallica cranked to pain threshold. The not-so-veiled conclusion of my report was that writing it had been a pointless exercise.

'This assessment,' the VPDP said, his eyes going blinky-blink. 'It's terrific. You're a sharp woman. We need a lot more of this, this kind of … what do you call it. Style?' He eyed my ribs. Then I was offered a promotion leading the new strategic assessment team, whose main responsibility was writing reports.

The rest of the afternoon I sat doubled over in a washroom stall, arms around my head in a cold and queasy funk. The person in the mirror did look like a consumptive waif when I finally emerged.

I phoned in sick the next day and decided to quit as soon as my new credit cards had been approved.

My dad reprimanded me. There were still bank loans.

I told him about some of the things I'd witnessed at work.

'Katherine,' he said, 'that's just how the world is. Would you rather have bombs in the streets?' He'd been running the local Re/Max office for decades and business was stable, but he'd gone through a rough patch back when my mother moved to Sweden with her new boyfriend, and I'd just begun university then. Now I owed the Royal Bank a haunting, five-digit sum.

'You'll pull through it,' Dad said.

That was just what I feared. I'd spent the last four years closely observing those who'd 'pulled through.'

I was still living in my inaugural Toronto apartment, where memories of my ex-boyfriend lingered along with the odorous meat my neighbours fried nightly. I wanted to be far away. I wanted to get in the car and drive for weeks and pass out of everything I'd known. I wanted distance to dig into me, to leave a thick, dried husk in my wake while I whizzed on, a small bright creature newly arrived in the world. As I lay on the couch for a week, this fantasy grew. I could see the luggage piled in the back seat, the creased Michelin guide. Where would I go? Where could I go, and still survive?

Pragmatism caught up with me. But then I thought of Vancouver: forests and white-peaked mountains, a sparkling city by the sea. I talked to my boss about my quandary, explained I'd been thinking of making a big move, you see, and so the promotion, though very flattering ... By the end she felt it had been her idea to put in a request for my transfer to the company's BC office in Burnaby. Which was almost Vancouver.

I was going west! The very word seemed synonymous with hope. Go west. Westward ho! Follow the setting sun. My summertime departure preparations hardly gave me time to think. I had going-away parties: an office do at which my co-workers snidely let me know that my exit from the flock was an unforgivable criticism; a dinner out with Dad, who didn't understand but was relieved there was a job waiting; sad, celebratory nights with friends. I was taking valerian to get to sleep. A contract arrived from Burnaby. The web site photo showed an office tower under a blue sky, the horizon obscured by a dark mass that most certainly was mountains.

II.

The first few days on the road I was still in a daze. Past Barrie, each town felt like an outpost. The highway narrowed, the roadside malls vanished.

I entered a slipstream of rocks and trees, the car seeming to steer itself past the highway signs, a floaty state of stillness in motion. Then a long stretch after Wawa where there was only a pine-forest sea, the highway an asphalt runnel through its midst like a miracle of Moses. And the great lake – that other sea – appearing below on my left, with its Precambrian shores and skimming insects of freighters, and the ancient icy water going far far down to lands without the sun.

Sentences would form as I drove, but I had no one to talk to. The scrawled-over napkins became a nuisance; the car became a shabby den. In Kenora I cleaned out the trash, bought a notebook and tried unsuccessfully to clarify my thoughts at the counter of a waterfront diner, where the freshest thing to eat was a pale tomato sandwich. Outside in the parking lot were dusty Ford pickups, their male owners lingering over midmorning coffees with a will that suggested no one would be missing them soon.

I thought my daze would vanish, but it didn't. The prairies rolled past like an ocean on which it seemed I'd been journeying for years, the occasional town an atoll rising and falling quickly behind, and I was seized by a strange, sea-born anxiety that I might not make the other side. I stopped sleeping, and when the Rockies finally reared on the horizon, I took them in a day.

The mountains were clouded – covered the whole ten hours I drove through them by thick clouds whose movements would suddenly expose a frozen sunlit peak or stately flank high above the road. And for the first time in my life I saw clouds being born, right there beside the highway. They puffed up like languid genies from branches and screes and drifted across the road as I stared in sleep-deprived wonder.

And then I was on the other side. Driving through green farm-land country again, a Dutch-school landscape of silos and sleepy pastures recessed from the hell-bent highway. Had a fatal turn short-cut me back to southwestern Ontario? The sun had set by the time rush-hour traffic spilled me out of the Fraser Valley and into Vancouver. From high on a bridge, a view of the city's streetlight grid under a darkening sky, a 7-11 sign by a distant curb. Four thousand kilometres from home, and the urban genre was still the same.

But a mountain with a brightly lit slope beckoned to the north. I drove toward it and arrived downtown, where I inched up Robson Street, trying to get an instant feel for the culture. Everything seemed very clean, including the people. I couldn't remember what it all reminded me of; a magazine, maybe. Neon shimmered in the long black hair of Asian women. The air was shimmering too, the cars and parking meters wavering, hologramic. I hadn't slept in over thirty-six hours.

The hostel was a bugger to find and awesome to behold: a great white building of some bygone institution on a lonesome beach across the bay from downtown. I checked in, stuffed my valuables into a locker and crawled under the sheets with such gratitude and obliterating fatigue that only as I was dropping to sleep did I realize the sound I was hearing was not the car engine, but waves falling and falling onto sand.

III.

The first person I met in Vancouver was a classical guitarist named Damien.

I was breakfasting near English Bay, in a café where everyone was dressed in hiking clothes. I'd put aside my maps and guidebooks and was examining a novel I'd found at the hostel when from behind me came the scrape of a chair leg and a tentative voice at my ear: 'Oh, J. G. Ballard. Do you like his stuff?' I turned and looked into a pair of dark eyes set in a ghostly face, its pallor emphasized by a black turtleneck. As soon as I responded the trap sprang: his chair came round and he leaned awkwardly over the arm in a pose of rapt attention. During the brief conversation that followed, Damien veered from Ballard to David Cronenberg to Fritz Lang to limited interaction theory and postmodern architecture, as if by ranging this far together we must become friends.

I mentioned my appreciation for Tárrega and Frescobaldi. Damien's large eyes brimmed. I felt, uncomfortably, like a mother duck whose duckling has just imprinted.

But when I inquired about the classical-guitar-playing life, his manner changed.

'There is no "living" to be made,' he said. 'There's too much competition. They keep *moving* here.' And he gestured toward the aspiring Segovias and Breams passing the window outside. 'It's worse and worse each year,' he added, pressing his forehead with the heel of his hand and scrunching his bangs. His fine hair was cut into one of those cheap, generic hairstyles for men – the 'short' style – with an off-centre cowlick that gave him a retro seventies look. The illegitimate Brady kid: weird, alone, chronically misunderstood.

'Well,' I offered, 'can one really expect a living from concerts and commissions anywhere? Isn't that rare? Surely most artists must also support themselves in other ways.'

'There aren't any concerts. Vancouverites don't give a shit about music. Under twenty-five and they're on Ecstasy dancing to electronic hoof clops. Under fifty-five they're all filmmakers and exercise freaks. Then they retire to look after ferns.'

I put this down to bitterness. Earlier that morning, I'd woken at the hostel to find glory incarnate: the sky was clear and boats scooted about the bay, their billowed sails bright with heraldic designs. All was action and energy: people jogging and dogs snuffing on the beach, choppy white-capped waves, and on the far shore but startlingly close rose the mountains, their blue-and-white ridges so emphatic against the sky that my heart leapt with expectation. Coffee in hand I'd stood on the beach gaping at my first view of the Pacific coast. With my stale, travel-wrinkled clothes and thumping heart, I'd felt like an explorer who's just hacked through the last bush and stepped into the breezy shock of the bay. I sniffed the air. The air was good. I opened my arms to the wind.

But now clouds had come. Low and thick, they sat over the coast like a false ceiling, hiding the mountains and crowding the city. I looked out at the bay, where freighters hulked like icebergs in the grey waves. Damien looked too, and together we watched as the first raindrops hit the panes and the world wavered, then blurred.

'The last concert I gave was at a twentieth wedding anniversary party,' he said. 'Everyone got loaded and wanted "Layla". Do you know what I read recently? A CD by an acclaimed classical guitarist at the height of his career can expect to sell eight hundred copies in North America.' He sighed. 'The world is changing.'

Then he noticed the guidebooks.

'Oh, you don't live here?' he asked, looking sad.

I hesitated. Intense and potentially unstable – certainly. But Damien was still the first person to enter my new life, and I fiercely wanted to be honest.

'I've been transferred here,' I said, and was immediately disappointed with myself. 'Very willingly,' I added, and I tried to explain about the shrinking work station and the washroom stall. I was determined, if embarrassed; in Ontario (which was all I knew), you don't share emotional histories on first meetings – often not in a lifetime, unless much alcohol is involved.

Damien was wildly sympathetic. He hoped that being in Vancouver would 'heal my brokenness'. Those were his words, and though I was grateful for them, they grated.

When I made motions to leave, he practically panted with anxiety. He would leave too, and walk up Denman Street too. And so he tagged along until, out of a desire to be alone yet have insurance against loneliness, I agreed to meet him again.

I walked back to the beach and squinted at the freighters.

It was Monday. I'd travelled across the continent to a new life and made a date with a wet blanket.

It was Monday, and I was scheduled to show up for an orientation meeting followed by a project brief at three o'clock. I needed more time.

At a pay phone I called the office and said there'd been car trouble. 'You can take a taxi,' the woman on the other end said. We're all in this grief together, her voice silently added.

Did I mention the car trouble happened in Revelstoke?

'I see,' she replied carefully. I pictured her telephone screen showing a Vancouver area code. Beside me, two gulls screeched over a piece of trash.

'I'll be there tomorrow first thing,' I said quickly, and hung up.

On Tuesday, I met my new co-workers and was handed several documents that my boss said had been targeted for revision by a program consultant: 'Western Canada Market Share Analysis', 'Oral Presentation Training for B-Level Employees', 'Environmental Impact Survey Tools and Procedures'. Tip of the pile.

At five o'clock I drove back to the hostel and moved over to the YWCA downtown. The commute took one hour, twenty-five minutes.

From seven to eight, I sensed I was about to experience a significant emotion. I lay on my narrow bed. Then I set the alarm and fell asleep.

The sleep I'd skipped on the highway caught up to me that week and I slept long and fitfully at the Y. I fell asleep in my office chair. Suspicions about the effects of Pacific weather on my Upper Canadian physiology formed: the rain clouds had come and the rain clouds had stayed, which people claimed was not *quite* normal for autumn. Softly, steadily, all through the days and nights the rain fell, until I felt caught in an endless, languorous kiss between ocean and sky. My impressions of the city mostly came from under an umbrella: gummed sidewalks, cement foundations, steps, signposts, soggy shoes. Shapes loomed beyond the car's foggy windows and the rilled panes of my office. My damp room at the Y felt like a ship's berth: I woke and turned through the night to the distant clanks and creaks of the elevator's cables, and the wet wind against the window.

Soon after our first meeting, Damien began calling me daily. It was often he who woke me up at work, serenading me on the phone with Spanish romances or tortuously complex pieces of his own composition. He took me to a fragrant Japanese tea house, where he dwelled on the frustrations of the artistic life, then, remembering himself, leaned perilously close and asked with great concern if I was 'surviving'.

I looked into the cup between my hands, where tea leaves swirled. 'I can't say I'm stressed,' I said. 'It's more like I can't think. Everything's dreamy. I feel like I'm not even really here, like I haven't arrived yet. Or that I'm waiting for something.' Damien looked like he wanted to make a confession, and I went quickly on. 'What do people do here? That's what I haven't figured out,' I said. 'The city core seems so small.'

Damien's brow furrowed. 'Do?'

'For fun. What's the thing?'

He puffed his cheeks and rolled his eyes. 'We're doing it. Unless you're into snowboarding or whatever.'

But he agreed to think about it, and over the next week we did something like a city tour. He took me for sushi and for *dim sum* in Chinatown, which only reminded me of Toronto. We walked the seawall in the rain. He took me into the Stanley Park Zoo, where I needed to leave after my first glimpse of a tourist crowd ogling caged, crazed monkeys. We sampled restaurants run by hippies, by feminists, by gays, by Eastern religious orders, even one run by communists, where we ate under a faded Che Guevara poster while the staff's numerous children ran around the room unchecked. As Damien and I spent more time together I concluded that my sexual attraction to him was low, which was probably for the best. Not that he was unattractive. I imagined that, as a youth, Damien had probably been beautiful. Now his mouth was a tense line; the beauty lay mainly in his hands, which were slim and elegant and strong, with perfectly shaped nails. Occasionally some enthusiasm would dispel his remorse and self-pity and his features would regain their boyish fullness. But even then my sexual radar sensed hidden, dangerous objects.

Nonetheless, I agreed to go to his place for dinner. My rain-cloud claustrophobia was growing, and Damien's intensity was something of a beacon.

Financial constraints had forced Damien to give up his apartment. He was now house-sitting for a well-off couple who attended church with his ex-wife and had gone overseas for a year. They had a strange home in a Frank Lloyd Wright style, a sprawling urban cottage with a colony of ceramic gnomes in the yard. Inside was a country kitchen with skirted chairs, doilies and yet more ceramic creatures. Damien practised guitar in the living room, slept on a daybed watched by the couple's cats, or paced the rooms in his black turtleneck and jeans like a bottled spirit.

Despite several preliminary phone calls, he was in a lather of stress when I arrived. Was I sure I wasn't allergic or intolerant? Was I fond of spices, okay with butter, thirsty, hungry, cold, hot or otherwise uncomfortable, bored, in a hurry to leave? But the meal, a poached salmon with dill and roasted vegetables, was lovely. We sat in candlelight with the cats jumping on and off the table and drank two bottles of wine. We laughed at the house. On impulse I retrieved some of the figurines and set them on the table.

'Okay, Damien. The gnomes are coming.' I slid two of the fat, pointy-hatted figures toward him. Damien sat with his mouth open, looking autistic. 'They're closing in. What are you going to do?' I reached for more figures. 'Damien, Damien, come join us,' I chanted, lining the gnomes into a semi-circle just beyond his plate. 'Damien!' I bounced the gnomes. 'Come with us!' I was now crouched with my face at table height. Damien seemed caught in a complex reaction. Finally I heard a small voice say, 'Where?'

'To gnome land!' I nosedived the figures off the table and into the cats' water dish. Silently Damien picked up a gnome and followed, accompanying its dive into the water with a long and spitty 'Splash!' We scrambled about on the floor poking gnomes behind curtains and under cushions and into flowerpots. There was a chase based on a plot that the wine has since erased. We ended up in an unlit hallway near the bedrooms. I stopped and sat back against the wall, but Damien was still on all fours.

'Gruff gruff,' he said, nosing his gnome along the carpet by my feet.

I stared at the red pointy hat.

'Gruff *gruff.*' The hat poked. The gnome slid up my shin to my knee. I put a hand on its head.

'Sorry,' I said. 'I need a rest.'

'So rest.' The gnome pushed a determined inch further.

'Damien –'

He pulled back and sat down beside me with a sigh. From an open window came the sound of rain. I stood and groped my way back to the kitchen.

IV.

My new workplace was familiar in a half-day, my co-workers indistinguishable in office attitudes and etiquette from their Toronto counterparts. Yet despite frequent napping I produced efficiently and spent mostly a natural amount of time in the washrooms. My dominant feeling – boredom – I interpreted positively; I'd decided that work was a kind of sleep, a departure into a state of understimulation, and this conviction pleased me. After all, what was wrong with sleep? The secured, cloudwreathed office tower was a sorcerer's castle that stole my days, but at least I was set joyfully free each evening to explore the city or read in my berth. I stayed up late. I discovered Vancouver's nineteenth-century skeleton, the sketchy remains of it: Gastown, small and touristy, was the largest chunk, a polished jawbone. Portside I found an iron footbridge, factories, warehouses that hummed in the night. Then there was nothing but a big black gap in time through which you fell for centuries into a cedar grove, where totemic faces evoked Greek myths and Egyptian deities, and none of these.

In a crowded sushi eatery early one such evening, a woman sitting next to me at the counter claimed that no one in Vancouver has relatives living in Vancouver. The woman was dressed in wet cycling gear;

she had thick, fuzzy braids of chestnut hair and a wispy, quite attractive moustache.

'Vancouver,' she said, chewing, 'is a spiritual destination.' Then, chopsticks paused, she peered at me with small, very blue eyes to see how this sank in.

I felt chilled. How did she know I was one of the possessed? An explorer-escapee driven by vague notions of salvation?

'What do you mean?' I said.

'You don't think it's true?'

I gave a startled look. 'I'm new here. I don't know.' I was slipping into my usual mode of polite dishonesty.

She was a charming, mysterious thing. She introduced herself as Glynnis, and as we were saying goodbye, she invited me to a party with what she called her 'tribe', who went by the name Cosmic Elfs. She said I'd just have to come to see what this meant.

Glynnis was only the second non-work person to begin a conversation with me in Vancouver. Thus far, people had struck me as oddly reserved. All waiting for the end of the rain, perhaps.

As I was walking along the waterfront after the sushi place, I went back to her statement about people in Vancouver having no relatives here. Damien, I recalled, was from a northern Manitoba town where one can hear ice *doing* things. Was Glynnis right? I decided to initiate a poll. It would provide a tool for meeting more people.

I came upon a sign for a walk-on ferry to Granville Island, which lay just across the water and wasn't an island at all, my guidebooks said. I thought the boat was a tourist trap, since the trip couldn't take more than five minutes, but the service is for real and is called the Aquabus. The ferry, a tug about the size of a minivan, contained one other passenger and tilted as I ducked on board. After a few minutes the driver ('captain' seems rather exalted) cast off and U-turned with a spin of the tiller, and we burbled downstream. The windows were fogged up, but he'd left the door open so I could watch the shoreline through the pelting rain, and the little wake of our passage spreading out from below the step.

My co-passenger sat slouched, regarding the driver with a sullen, inward stare. His clothes were wet and there were drops of rain on his glasses. When I looked over, he said, 'Nice weather.'

'I keep hearing people say it's unusual.'

'Where are you from?'

'Toronto. Where are you from?' I said, initiating my poll.

'Iraq.'

'Oh.'

The Aquabus was already nearing Granville Island, passing the slick stumps of a skeleton pier. I was thinking about war-ruined cities, mint tea, desert plains and streets the colour of sand; all that, and then this marine metropolis. I felt the man looking at me.

'Sohrob,' he said, holding out a hand.

He began asking when I'd arrived, why I'd arrived, et cetera. I said I was in Vancouver for 'complicated personal reasons' and flipped the conversation over to his story. We disembarked and walked up the plank. His English was better than most Canadians', though he'd been here only five years. As we strolled through the empty farmers' market building, I learned that he hated his programming job though loved computers, and that he'd never been anywhere but Baghdad, Vancouver and Winnipeg, where by some twist of fate his immigrating family had landed and his parents had incomprehensibly settled (but Sohrob couldn't stay there, he felt the westward pull too). My questions seemed to please him and he grew more personal. His parents were engineers, he their only 'great hope' child. I thought I could see maternal over-indulgence in his coffee-stained shirt and round belly, his scuffing, hands-in-jacket-pockets walk. He declared himself a pessimist, as if this were a creed. Human nature itself had failed to progress from even the most primitive days; only technology allowed us the luxuries of compassion and comfort. When we emerged onto the street he invited me to coffee, yet, fearing this might be another incarnation of Damien, I resisted.

It didn't matter. Within the hour I ran into him on Granville Street, back on the other side of the water.

I was developing a theory that Vancouver has even more coffee shops than Toronto. There seemed to be one Starbucks per block downtown and on every corner was a competitor and they were *all* busy. People just walked around with umbrellas and coffee cups.

I mentioned this to Sohrob when we met for coffee after work. He nodded thoughtfully and explained that caffeine is responsible for the rise of the modern technological society because it enables the intensified mental activity needed to drive invention and production in an information-based economy; and Vancouver, as the newest big city in the world, has the shallowest history and thus the weakest resistance to modern forces. 'So,' he concluded, lighting a cigarette, 'we're the worst caffeine heads.' Which was going a bit far, I thought.

'Isn't the strongest coffee in the world in places like Somalia, or the Middle East?' I said.

'Sure, but there it's connected to social ritual.'

'Which isn't what's happening now?'

Sohrob grinned, showing the bottoms of tiny, crooked teeth behind thin lips. I'd yet to see him laugh, but he grinned a lot, especially when talking about something bad – which was most of the time. 'Yeah, we're all just extensions of the machine now,' he'd say, eyes full of pleasure, a jolly citizen of the *noir* coffeehouse.

It had stopped raining when we got outside. Not for the first time: the rain *had* ceased occasionally, but clouds still covered the sky and the air was damp, so even when it was not raining there was the threat of rain, the drippy, recent *presence* of rain. Sohrob suggested we get my car so he could show me 'the overlooked details' of the city. We drove down Seymour Street and stared at bored-looking hookers pacing the sidewalks, tarty but quite alluring poised atop their stiletto tips like determined ballerinas, all grit and grace. We rolled down long alleyways canopied with hydro poles and wires. Emerging onto Burrard Street, I let traffic take us over the bridge into Kitsilano, past stucco and cedar-board houses hidden by gardens, fruit trees, sprawling shrubs and slick arbutuses, which I'd just learned to recognize. Green mould lined the houses' shingles and grooves. Everything was steaming, verdant. The land still had a voice you couldn't ignore and it seemed possible to be happy.

I remarked to Sohrob how strange Canada must have been when he arrived.

He shrugged. 'We were glad to leave Iraq.'

'But didn't it, doesn't it still freak you out?' I veered onto Marine Drive and we curved down a dreamy wooded bend until the hostel appeared. 'The thought that you've left everything behind,' I went on. 'All the people, all the history, all your culture.' He didn't react. 'Your childhood. Your fucking language, for God's sake. I mean, how does it … shit, Sohrob! Nothing will ever be the same.' I looked at him, but he was watching the beach roll past.

'It's all just gone.' I tried to snap my fingers, but my hand fell back on the wheel. Only three weeks since I'd seen and touched my friends or heard the local streetcar's rumbling glide as I lay in bed. Only three weeks and already my former life seemed as irrevocable as an object dropped in water. Friends had promised to visit in the New Year, while I couldn't project myself into next month. I'd done nothing to find a home. I still drew from my Toronto bank.

Sohrob turned to me. 'It's not as big a deal as you think,' he said.

I glanced at him dubiously.

'Iraq is a medieval country. I don't even want to go back.'

'What – never?'

In response he lifted one hand in a gesture that seemed both dismissive and self-protecting.

We drove on, climbing into the forested lands surrounding the university. The road angled south. Water appeared to the west. Parking the car, we found a viewpoint and stood looking down at the ocean, where freshly cut timber floated in neat squares.

'That's Wreck Beach over there,' Sohrob said.

'Huh?'

'*Nudists*,' he explained.

'Really?' I craned to see. I thought it might be beautiful to be naked there, beyond sight of the city.

'Ever been to it?' I asked.

'Yeah. Right.'

'Why not?'

He dragged on his cigarette. 'Because I have a job,' he said, like this was a side chosen.

We drove straight back downtown and parted at a Skytain Station with a vague agreement to do coffee again sometime. I watched him disappear up the stairs. Soon the driverless train came gliding out of the station, steered along its viaduct route by unseen forces, distant software and coffee-drinking technicians. Thinking of Sohrob hunkered down in a seat, a takeout hit of brew in hand, I did find it hard to imagine him anywhere else.

V.

I decided to go to Glynnis's Cosmic Elf party and to take Sohrob and Damien with me. But I didn't tell them about each other. I arranged to pick them up at home and drove to the Gnome House first.

I hadn't seen Damien since our dinner and was startled by his new, more sexually brazen look: snug black jeans and an Italian shirt, mauve, its open top buttons exposing a tangle of dark hair. His hair, combed straight back from his forehead and heavily gelled, gleamed like a helmet.

'Damien!' I smiled. 'Well look at you.'

'What?' he said innocently.

'You're all dressed up.'

He scowled as he pulled on a leather jacket. 'Men do anything different and they attract a crowd of scrutineers.'

We barely spoke in the car. Damien drummed his fingers and joggled his leg as if he couldn't wait to get to the party.

'Something on your mind?'

'Yes.'

'What?'

'I don't want to discuss it here.'

With this looming over us, we pulled up in front of Sohrob's building. He was waiting under a concrete overhang. I tooted the horn.

'Who's that?'

'A friend of mine who's coming to the party with us. You'll need to let him in the back seat.'

I made the introductions as we sped off and did nothing to dispel the appalled silence that followed.

'Sohrob helps make robotic limbs,' I said after a while. 'And Damien plays the guitar.'

'You're in a band?'

There was a snort.

I was coasting down Broadway Avenue, trying to read addresses through the rain. 'This isn't a *rave*, is it?' Damien said.

'I – hey! There's Glynnis.'

She was cycling almost beside us on a mountain bike decorated with plastic flowers. I pulled to the curb up ahead and got out, and Sohrob after me.

Glynnis stopped. I'd figured before that she was about my age, but she looked very girlish in her bicycling helmet. Her long braids were beaded with shiny drops.

'Kathy!' She threw her arms around my neck.

'You remember me?' I was flattered and charmed. Perhaps this eccentric woman would become the insightful female friend I'd so been missing here.

'Of course I do! Were you looking for the party? It's been cancelled. It's such a bummer! The whole tribe was converging. We couldn't swing the space though, 'cause the dancers needed it. So Sarah and Tex and have gone to return the equipment and my friend Katrina's in transit from Pender and I can't reach her, it's just so screwed up, and –' Much more information about people and places we didn't know followed.

The car was running with Damien still in it, a dark smudge against the window, and Sohrob and I were getting wet. I suggested we go to a bar, but Glynnis said she hated them. She wanted to sit on the beach.

'In this weather?' Sohrob said.

'So what?' She gave him a challenging smile.

I explained that the rest of us weren't dressed appropriately for the beach. But though each one of them lived alone, none wanted to have us over; the suggestion seemed to create stress. In the end I loaded Glynnis's bike in the trunk and headed for the Y. It was verging on ten o'clock and we had to sneak up through a back stairwell to avoid security. Once in my room I locked the door and rolled a towel into the gap. Damien began to scrutinize my toiletries, books, photographs and mail, while Sohrob went to the window and surveyed the grey cityscape beyond.

'Look! You can see the Skydome from here.' He pointed to the white, rubbery structure that loomed like a giant diaphragm beyond the expressway.

'How inspiring,' Glynnis said, dropping her wet cycling jacket and helmet on the floor. She sat on the bed and rolled off her socks, wiping wet lint from her feet.

Sohrob took the chair that went with the desk and Damien hovered by the wall behind him. I handed out doubles of Scotch in plastic cups and squeezed beside Glynnis, who sat cross-legged in the centre of the bed. We raised our glasses in a mute toast and drank. Someone's cup crinkled.

Glynnis said, 'So, what brought you to the coast, Kathy?' There was a distinctive pride in her intonation of the phrase 'to the coast' – as if it were not merely a place to live, but an enlightened way of being. I went through the explanation of my move; it was getting briefer each time I said it. Then, in roundtable fashion, Sohrob and Damien and Glynnis related their 'born and fled' stories.

People's eyes cast about the room. 'No TV,' Sohrob observed.

'Thank God for that,' Glynnis said.

'So what's your tattoo?' he asked. Reclining on her elbows, she stretched out a leg to show us the small yin-yang symbol in black and red above her ankle. We leaned in. Sohrob asked if she had others.

'That's a rather intimate question,' she coyly replied.

'Okay. Why yin-yang?'

Glynnis thought for a moment. She became serious, and when she spoke she addressed us each in turn. I felt an uncomfortable urge to goggle my eyes whenever her steady gaze fell on me. 'Well,' she began, 'it's a personal symbol, as it must be since I've chosen to have it engraved on my body. It's connected to a lot of my core beliefs about who I am and who we are collectively, that we all contain the so-called male and female elements and that we need to understand and accept this about ourselves. In fact, our ignorance and fear of our own nature are killing this planet –'

'You really think our problems are that simple?' Sohrob said.

'I didn't say they were simple.' Glynnis stared, clearly annoyed. 'But in one sense, yes, I think they are. A basic sense.'

'Katherine says you're some kind of activist.'

'No I didn't.'

'Sure you did. You said it sounded like a save-the-world party.'

My face reddened. The Scotch, the crowded room, the damp smells from our clothes and shoes, were fuelling a growing desire to dispense with nicety. 'I was hypothesizing. I had no information. I was referring to the Cosmic Elfs, which I still don't know about.'

'Elfs?'

Glynnis merely smirked.

'Some very interesting people she knows, too interesting to define,' I said.

Damien spoke. 'So do you think everyone is actually bisexual?'

We looked at him. His cowlick was resisting the gel, and two pointy licks of hair hung down, framing his forehead.

'Well I am,' Glynnis said. She stared at us boldly.

Sohrob grinned. He was slouching in his chair with his glass on his belly, watching Glynnis as you would a TV show. 'So that's part of it, I suppose?'

'What do you mean 'part of it'?'

'Yin-yang, the personal philosophy you're wearing. You're bisexual, so naturally that's part of how you see reality. Everyone's philosophy comes from what's real to them. But I'm heterosexual, so naturally I have a philosophy that totally disagrees with yours. I don't mean you're *wrong*, any more than I'm wrong. It's subjective. The world's a mirror, all you ever see is yourself and you call it truth.'

Glynnis's eyes had grown brighter. She started gesticulating.

'First of all, I wasn't being that literal. Secondly, the 'subjective' argument is just the kind of solipsistic, relativist position that people use as an excuse to disengage with life and keep themselves isolated, thus leading to apathy, misery and negligence toward themselves and the planet. But the thing is –'

'But I *like* being isolated,' Sohrob said, turning to me with a grin.

'If you'd get involved –'

'I like it!'

'– you'd see the commonalities instead of –'

'– that's me, that's my point! I'm a misanthrope. I want –'

'Oh really? So you're happy then, you're not just a tad cynical and lonely and depressed? And you think –'

'I don't want some concerned "community" wondering how I feel. That's why I live in a cold, anonymous city. If I wanted engagement I would have stayed with my family –'

'– refusing to acknowledge the connectedness, the people and resources that –'

Damien jumped in. 'She's right! It's a fantasy of –'

'Your isolation is a grand illusion, my friend, the classic, classic, male self-deception and warped dream –'

'– where I was driven insane, I mean TOTALLY fucking nuts. You have no idea of the constraints even in a comparatively non-traditional –'

'– which can't be worse than –'

'– a concoction of the elite –'

'You need to keep your voices down. Can we please –'

'– give anything to just –'

'– hallway security. Hallway security can –'

'– because the problem is that we get our first taste, that proto-community experience, from our families, where –'

'BE QUIET.'

'You're classic, just totally classic,' Glynnis muttered.

I rose and picked up the bottle.

When I reached Damien his brow was creased with concern. His fingers touched my arm in a semi-caress that made Glynnis stare. 'You okay?' he whispered, though everyone could hear.

'Of course I am.' I picked up his hand and pressed it back to him with a passion I hadn't intended.

Glynnis declined the bottle. Reaching in her knapsack, she pulled out a baggie of dope and rolling papers and started constructing a joint. Sohrob was hunched over, brooding into his cup. Damien beckoned me to follow him to the door.

'What?'

'I have to talk to you about something.'

'Now?'

He glanced back at the others. 'It's about this.'

'Can I smoke in here?' Sohrob said.

'It's a non-smoking building. I could take you down the stairwell and let you back in.'

'Can we go up to the roof?' Glynnis asked, getting up to slide open the long window that spanned the end of the room. In came damp, exhaust-scented air and the sound of swishing tires. Sohrob leaned toward her and said something I couldn't hear.

Damien whispered to me. 'Katherine, I've been thinking that this really isn't necessary.'

'This?'

'Room. Listen, you could stay with me. I've got the place for another six months and there's lots of space, totally free.'

'Oh. That's –'

'No. Don't dismiss it.' With his hand on my shoulder he bent closer, his eyes very soft. 'It could be whatever arrangement you want, you see? I have no expectations. Honestly. You know, I once slept in the same bed for weeks with a woman I was really attracted to, and nothing happened.'

'Really?'

'Yes. Anything's possible.'

To such an assertion, there seemed no reply. I felt remote and foreign, a player on the wrong stage.

I excused myself and went into the washroom. There was a pain inside me: homesickness. But I didn't yearn for Toronto or even my hometown, though I did miss the house I grew up in, with its elm tree and wild grape in the yard, all sold in the divorce. Mostly, though, it was some imaginary home I longed for. It really felt like I'd been there once, lived there. I picked up *The House at Pooh Corner* from the bathroom counter and sat down.

It seemed to me that I no longer had an age. I was ageless, in the sense that my age did not correspond, socially or historically, to any stage for an individual in a culture I knew of. Adult, yet immature; fertile, yet without a spouse; independent, but aimless. Had I really matriculated? Passed grade seven? Such accomplishments, made with so little awareness, amazed me. I had no ideas, no plans, and worst of all, I'd discovered no true calling for myself. I'd just been playing out a life from a script handed out somewhere back in grade school. A neatly typed document smelling of photocopier chemicals, with no colour illustrations, no cloth cover frayed from love. A document that came from the teacher's desk. The first words were a command: You must. And the last were a warning: Don't fail.

But I'd fled all the way to the perimeter now, started over.

No, I'd not even begun. I'd been floating, waiting to feel solid ground. And maybe it wasn't going to happen. Maybe I'd have to seek it. Yet how?

I sniffed, wiped my nose with toilet paper. Deep inside myself, through the thicket of education, parental constraints and half-baked notions of propriety, I felt a fierce throb of authentic desire, that vulnerable, potent core I kept trying to return to in my long washroom-stall escapes at work.

I emerged into the room. Glynnis greeted me enthusiastically, like I'd just arrived to the party, and ushered me into the tight space between the bed and the window where they were grouped.

I looked outside. Rain was falling on the expressway that I took to work. I felt wide awake, sharp, and I wanted to stay that way.

I said, 'I think I might quit my job.'

'And do what?' Sohrob asked.

I turned around.

'Who cares?' Glynnis said. 'Quitting work is great! Yay.'

Damien looked at me. 'You seem really sad.'

'Well I'm not.'

Glynnis laughed. Suddenly she stepped forward and embraced me.

'It's okay, Kathy, we're your friends.'

I stiffened, aghast.

'Relax, relax,' she cooed. 'Damien, Sohrob, get in here.'

'I don't do group hugs,' Sohrob said.

'Me neither.'

'Now you do. Kathy needs it.' Glynnis grabbed their arms and yanked them in. Sohrob's shoulder crushed my nose. I smelled deodorant. Glynnis held me tightly, my arms pinned at my sides. I wriggled one free and reached across Damien's waist, which felt very slim, almost like my own. With my other hand I touched Sohrob's nylon jacket. His heavy arm crossed my back. Someone's knee, I think Damien's, dug into my thigh. My eyes had closed. And then the warm damp grip, which left no room for resentments, began to circulate the human energy of our four bodies, and we started to sway.

Lawless

In his seventh year at TrendCorp, Dayton began to disappear. The world, though, didn't seem to notice.

'It's my right arm.'

He held it out for the doctor. Sleeved, the arm looked normal enough, if rather thin from lack of exercise. Dayton was one of those men who lose weight when out of shape, and it had been months since he'd given up weights and morning runs for more smoking and work. Now a driving glove masked the problem hand. With hope and dread, Dayton tugged at the leather fingertips. Only desperation, steadied by a triple Scotch, had enabled him to leave home, to sit with others in the clinic's dour waiting room aware that his condition, if confirmed, might cast him out from even this simplest, ordinary community.

The dermatologist's face loomed over his hand, eyes peering through thick, practical glasses. Except where his hand and wrist should have been Dayton saw only an empty space. He hadn't lost the actual feeling of the hand. He could verify its warmth and solidity, the light-wire hair of his knuckles. But its visibility was vanishing – gradually, and somewhat unevenly, like a pond drying up through a drought. The tips of his index finger and thumb floated on their own now, disconnected, like two last puddles.

The doctor tucked in her chin and eyed him over the spectacles' rim. 'I see nothing like the rash you described,' she said.

'What do you see?'

She prodded him with a metal stylus. 'Normal, healthy tissue.'

Dayton stared dully through his palm at the tiled floor. *Psychological disorder:* he felt the foreign and distressing words in his gut, like he'd swallowed metal.

Exactly when the problem started Dayton couldn't have said, since he was so busy these days he barely had time to feed, let alone examine, his body. But he first noticed something on a Monday morning two weeks ago when he was washing his hands in the men's room: a pale, white patchiness on his fingers. He put it down to the cold office air and held his hands under the hot water for an extra minute, rubbing them vigorously under the dryer afterwards.

The TrendCorp office hummed. Reentering its grey halls, Dayton felt a static prickling on his skin. Even the dust here was electrified, microbic and human chafings that had drifted into computer equipment and danced among the dark circuitry until vented like sparky pollen. The network, expanded over the years, now traversed every office, meeting room and hallway with its cables and printers, PC's and nodes. The air had a chlorinated tang.

Shares of TrendCorp, a modest Vancouver company that developed robotic limbs, had risen several years ago in value sufficiently to attract a large US corporation, which had swallowed Trend and in turn been swallowed by a multinational whose head office was located in a Chinese city of ten million, whose name no one at Trend had never heard of or could say. The effects of these changes were perceived by staff more on a spiritual than material level, in the sense that the company owners, who in the old days held management meetings and biannual retreats, ascended into the realm of overseas data transmissions. There was an important person called Mr Ong. And a woman named Xian-call-me-Janet. But aside from the consolidation of departments and inevitable staff adjustments, work at Trend had continued much the same. Dayton, who was part of the original management group that included John and Brad, still oversaw R&D. Every deadline was critical, every project demanded all they had.

Back in his office, Dayton resumed typing. In walked Brad, with eyes like two burnt holes. He was chugging a Coke. 'We're fucked,' he said. He belched, his eyelids lifting in mild surprise then resuming their grim, saurian weight. 'Ong's demanding z-node by this afternoon. If we don't submit by next Friday, Dallas will. They're that close.'

Dayton glanced down at this keyboard, this brief movement signalling that Brad's message had been received.

'John's totally freaked,' Brad said.

John is a *freak*, thought Dayton.

Brad wandered over to the window. The office floor vibrated, stopped. After a moment he finished his pop then went off, muttering 'We're fucked.'

Over the next few days Dayton noticed that the patchiness on his skin was getting worse. Right side first, a splatter of dime-sized marks that enlarged and spread like mould up his hand and arm. Fingering the flat spots had no effect: nothing swelled, oozed, ached, peeled or bled. Allergy? Eczema? Dayton made a mental note to call someone next week and slid back into the lines of program code he was finalizing for Trend's patent application. When the discoloration crept up his shoulder to the base of his neck, he remembered an old colleague with vitiligo, a pigment disorder that turns people spotty, like calico cats. Michael Jackson had it, or claimed to.

Dayton wasn't vain, but he didn't want to look abnormal. Well, perhaps he was a little vain; he was quite attractive in a small-eyed, boyish-blond way, more stylishly groomed and dressed than many men in the tech industry, wearing his hair in a trendy, tousled cut. At thirty-five he'd grown thin sideburns that he trimmed every other morning. So when the spots neared his neck, something had to be done. He was lifting the phone to call his wife for the number of her dermatologist when his admin assistant, Annette, came in bearing a courier package. Smiling, she laid it on his desk with a few softly spoken words. Dayton spun in his chair and held out his hand. 'Hey Annette, ever seen anything like this?'

'What's that?' She bent closer and, to his surprise, touched his hand with her cool fingers. Her skin was the colour of powdered cocoa. Her neat nostrils had no visible hair inside. 'Bit of flakiness,' she said in her lilting, Caribbean voice. 'You need some moisturizer, Day.'

'No no, I mean the spots, these big white spots.' He pointed to them, nervously laughing. 'I don't think it's contagious, but they're all up my arm. Weird, eh?'

Annette didn't see any spots.

Neither, that evening, did his wife, Lynne. Both women gave him looks he didn't like at all.

That night he sat up late in his home office, smoking, examining his arm under the lamp. What did it mean? A nervous breakdown? That seemed unlikely. Marriage was good, kids good, income well into six figures and climbing. Stress, then? Bullshit. He didn't believe in the evils of stress. These days stress was overstressed. Pressure produced energy, energy growth, growth success, and success satisfaction.

There was nothing to do but return to work, yet the problem quickly worsened. Spots appeared on his legs. He became covered head to toe and still Lynne did not notice, not even when he presented himself naked in the kitchen one evening ('Day! The kids are still up!'). At work he'd started losing momentum, spending hours on the Internet searching for similar symptoms or under such depressing key words as 'madness' and 'hallucinations'. Preparing for bed one dismal night, he noticed that the original, oldest spots had changed: they were glossy now, almost light-reflective, and felt squishy. Panicked, Dayton raced downstairs to his laptop and looked up the symptoms of flesh-eating disease – which didn't match his own. Nor did he seem to have any cancer or parasite or vision problem referenced in the data-well of cyberspace. Wide awake and determined to stay sensible, he finished some edits on the patent revisions and e-mailed them to Ong. Then he found Lynne's Palm Pilot and the number of her dermatologist, and keyed it into his Palm Pilot with a note to call first thing.

The next morning, his life fell to pieces.

Lynne had taken the kids to school early, and he was eating breakfast alone at the kitchen table, examining his splayed fingers. Check: odd shiny patches still there – but hold on, this was new. On the knuckle of his baby finger, the shiny skin had returned to being white and firm, yet with a scabby-looking spot in the middle. Dayton picked at it. Alarmed, he bent closer: the scab had moved. He was sure. And another thing: it had a bit of gooey red stuff on it, and this was because the scab wasn't *on* his hand at all but *underneath* it – on the white table, where it had fallen, a stray crumb with jam, from his plate of toast.

With a cry Dayton leapt up and rushed into the living room. At the leather sofa he flattened his hand: the knuckle went black. Showed taupe against the carpet, green-veined at the spider plant, and paisley against his tie. Dayton collapsed into an armchair, his lips moving in mute plea to the room's stolid array of objects.

He had a *hole* in his hand. A FUCKING HOLE. Neat and clean, like a punch through plastic.

After a while he rose and shuffled toward a photo of his family: sure enough, when he pressed his hand to the glass Lynne's smiling face appeared, as if embedded in his very skin.

Traffic inched through Stanley Park. Seen from a bird's eye above, a link-chain pulleyed through the trees and stretched over the bridge to the mountainous northern shore, while a parallel chain moved in the opposite direction toward the grey delta of downtown, where trees and plots of land stood as islands offering slim refuge for the likes of birds. Now, Dayton thought as he lay on the couch, he might be coming home from work in his Intrepid, arcing across the bridge and up to his perch on the mountainside. He hadn't been out of the house in a week. And his son was staring at him.

'Please stop it, Jason. I'm sick.'

'How come when we're sick we have to stay in our rooms?'

'Because that's what Mom and me decided.' Dayton laid a dry hand across his forehead. 'Why don't you go play basketball outside?'

Jason's mouth sagged. He was nine, and this year he'd started putting his father into ironic quotes. 'Uh, like, maybe because it's been raining all day, "Dad," and it's, like, freezing outside, "Dad."'

Life was a nightmare: daily, Dayton's flesh had ebbed away as he lay under a blanket in the bleary rec room, red-eyed and unshaven, trying to calm himself with DVDs and video games – to rest – yet helplessly bracing, he felt, for whatever fate the indifferent universe was hurtling toward him. The dermatologist's visit put him off seeking any more outside help. His story was science fiction; he would be drugged and confined, his family and colleagues notified. Even when, if, his skin returned to normal, the rest of his life would be changed forever.

The controlled logic of the delusion, as he told himself it must be, humbled yet at times fascinated him. Naked before the bathroom mirror, Dayton saw his cock, still unaffected, sticking out stubbily from its nest; above hung his navel pegged in air, and higher up the cirrus wisps of chest hairs floated. Most of his torso was gone, receding toward the solar plexus. The effect made him seem taller, his head like a larger planet beyond the satellites of stomach and groin.

During the day he sometimes paced about the empty house. Hadn't he been careful and good? Yet he'd become a suffering man, and neither his mind nor his spirit could discover a way out. The house was full of sounds that at times seemed capable of granting assurance, and he found himself listening attentively to the tones of fridge and furnace, air and jacuzzi filters, electric lights. A television's mutter, the dishwasher's heavy slosh. Or sometimes it was the call of an incoming plane he heard, one long, descending note. In lucid moments he phoned Brad, or did a little work if he could. He anxiously missed the office, knew his absence might derail the critical patent application they were rushing to complete. In the evenings, he slunk into the basement and hid. Jennie, his daughter, brought down cartons of orange juice and schoolwork and Lynne's basal thermometer for him to try, because she liked the way it bleeped, while Jason alternated between sweet and sullen attempts to gain attention. He took up the thermometer's sound as a kind of mockery song he used to announce his stomping arrivals and departures from the basement. *Meep. Meep-meep. Meep. Meep-meep.* Whenever his family came around Dayton wanted them gone, though sometimes as he lay alone, listening to them moving around upstairs, he would curl up and shake with tight hot sobs.

There was a transparent spot in his skull.

He put on a hat. He shaved, as if he were going out somewhere, as if nothing were wrong. But like the ozone hole over Antarctica, the spot grew. In a single day, his torso disappeared. His face. Only his cock remained, lewdly hanging there like some synthetic sex store item.

When Lynne arrived home from work to find her husband still basement-bound and morose, she tried some tough love. This was an unacceptably strange and dire flu: he must go to the hospital.

Dayton roused himself. 'No, it's okay. I'm seeing my doctor tomorrow,' he said.

'You are?' She approached the couch and knelt, making a sound he loved: the swish of skirt against pantyhose. 'I hope he gives you a round of antibiotics,' she said. 'Why don't you sleep upstairs tonight? I miss you.'

'I do too.'

'Day,' she said, and her voice changed; she was about to say something tricky. 'What is it really? There's something else wrong. I mean, not physical.' Dayton touched her face. Shallow indentations appeared on her cheeks.

'Please tell me,' she said, lowering her eyes. 'It's better to know, if you've done something you're ashamed of, or whatever it is. I'd rather deal with it than have you like this.'

If only. But why not just tell her then? Maybe he needed to hold on a bit longer to normal life, to be able to look in his wife's eyes and see there only the workday fatigue and average concern. He assured her there was nothing unusual. 'I'm just dead tired, beyond burnt out,' he said. 'I've been working like crazy.'

'I know.' She sighed and was quiet for a moment. 'What should we do about the party?'

Dayton hesitated. The party, their tenth wedding anniversary celebration, was scheduled for this weekend. The planning of it had long been a major principality of Lynne's, a realm of headspinning, bureaucratic detail. No, cancelling wouldn't be necessary, he murmured, then held out his arms so she crawled onto the couch and flattened herself against him. They slept. Later in the night he woke up alone. If he went to the mirror now and removed his clothes, would there be anything left to see? Hugging himself, repeating a mantra of *pleases*, Dayton lay in the TV's blue light, his wife's bottled scent on his hands.

* * *

Dayton's phone rang. Brad.

'You're up! Good. We're in deep shit. Fucking Virus Warning virus corrupted John's hard drive last night and I can't get into mine. You need to e-mail me the files. No wait. You need to ... Shit. This is so fucked. Are you there?'

Naked, Dayton was standing in the second-floor hallway under one of the home security system's wall boxes, watching its green light blink whenever he moved. The red light remained steady.

Sometime in the night, his cock had disappeared.

He'd been watching the security lights all morning.

'Brad,' he said, cutting into his colleague's babble. His own voice sounded different to him, more resonant, as if it were coming from further down. 'Tell John to deal with this.'

'John can't because his –'

'Yes, he *can*.'

Dayton hung up. He looked down. Though he couldn't see it, he could feel the return of the huge wodging hard-on he'd woken up with. He felt extraordinary: when he'd gazed into the mirror this morning and seen nothing, not one hair or nail, not even those twin dots of light where his pupils should be, he'd experienced a free-fall whoosh. But he didn't fall, or even cry out. Had he at last been driven over the edge, beyond the point of caring? Was this insanity? Around and around he'd turned before the mirror, raising his arms or a leg, parting his buttocks. Finally he'd gone upstairs into the morning, feeling a surprising lightness.

He decided to take a shower.

What a peculiar experience! The water seemed to be alive: it pooled around the empty spaces of his feet and sparked off his transparency in silvery sprays, it foamed about the hollow core of his fist at the nozzle. Long, twisting rills hung in air. Under soapy film the contours of his body were revealed and rinsed away, and when he soaped his erection and came, a pearly loop of semen fell on his arm and floated, it seemed. Dayton tasted it. The tang tingled on his tongue, spark of life.

Lynne arrived home that evening to find her husband dressed and preparing supper. He moved slowly in the kitchen, doing tasks by touch and starting to use his wedding ring and wristwatch to help judge distances. It was like adjusting to sudden blindness, he thought, but much easier.

He was so glad to see her. She put her arms around him and squeezed.

'Feeling better?'

'A little. Yes.'

'Thank God.' His hands slid under her sweater and she made pleased noises. 'I've got to go pick up the kids,' she whispered, detaching herself. But she gave him a long kiss before she went.

In their bedroom that night she was pretending to read, but he noticed the black nightgown she knew he loved. As he approached in his underwear, Dayton caught a brief, unsettling glimpse of himself in the window and was reminded of a Dr Seuss story he used to read to the kids ... something about a pair of pants with no one inside them. He giggled. Lynne, thinking he was focused on her, smiled and tossed aside her book.

Dayton was an average lover, with a tendency to be easily distracted and, sometimes when Lynne was in charge, to fall asleep. They still enjoyed friendly sex, though after more than a decade of monogamy, passion itself had become the stuff of kid-free vacations. Now, as soon as Dayton got into bed he found himself mashing his mouth against Lynne's breasts and running his hands eagerly all over her body, as if he hadn't touched her in months instead of weeks. He yanked off her nightgown and slid down to taste her, grunting as he burrowed with his tongue, and when at last he was inside her and looked down there she was: writhing on the bed beneath him as if in solo ecstasy – he her dream lover, the god-spirit entering her like a gust of wind. He lifted her breasts, repositioned her; she appeared to do these things herself, as if acted upon by his thoughts alone.

Dayton woke before dawn to the sound of humming. When he raised his ear from the pillow the sound stopped, became audible again with his head lowered. It sounded deep and faraway and mechanical, like the shielded heart of the city. Sleeping, Lynne stretched out a leg and toed his calf. In the grey light of their room Dayton rose, passed the digital clock and moved into the bathroom, where he urinated sitting down and then thoroughly scrubbed his hands and face, using a brush for the nails, rotating a washclothed finger in the oily corners of his nose. One verifying look at the room's reflection in the vanity mirror and he refocused on his tasks. The lovemaking with Lynne came back to him. He felt restless and horny, as if after a fast he'd consumed flesh instead of merely tasting it. He wanted to work and to fuck, but not in that order. Padding back to the bed, he stared down at Lynne and placed his hand on her shoulder.

He felt the urge to scratch her, so he could watch the long, red welts slowly appear on her skin.

On a fresh Monday morning Dayton returned to Trend, doing everything the usual way, only a little slower and more deliberately, that worked fine, and so, wearing a Prada suit and overcoat, he parked underground at seven-fifteen and headed up to the building's street-level coffee shop, which bombarded him with 'Jive Talking' as he entered. Several customers at various stages of being serviced stood waiting for the so-called *barrista,* an aproned girl of about seventeen who was singing along as she filled a steel jug with frothy milk. Dayton took his place in line.

'Hi there!' the girl said, tilting her head at him from behind the espresso machine.

Dayton looked at her. She wasn't pretty. Nonetheless he gave her a wide, relaxed smile. The smile had appeared on his face as he was dressing on Saturday evening for his anniversary party, inserting cufflinks into cufflink slits, looping and knotting a silk tie. He'd worn the smile as he welcomed his guests, the proud lord of the manor. 'Fantastic,' 'rejuvenated,' 'younger than ever' – everyone had looked at him with pleasure, incredulous that he'd been sick.

Now the coffee girl was doing it. 'How are you today?' she said.

'Absolutely wonderful.'

'Just a grande house blend for you today?'

Dayton thanked her, and the girl put down the jug, poured his coffee and brought it to the counter. He moved to the cash to pay.

In his office Dayton found a pile of files on his desk and guessed that the blinking light on the phone signalled yet more voice mails from Brad and John, those two interminable fuck-ups. They'd come to his anniversary party, stayed long, and eaten and drunk much, yet he, Dayton, had been the one to refine the patent application in time to beat their American competitor. He, Dayton, had saved their asses once again – despite all he'd been through.

Dayton stared out his south-facing window at the office tower across the street. He'd never liked this view.

Annette came in, hugging herself. 'Day! You're back!'

He turned around, startled. Here was this luscious young female, squishing her breasts together and smiling at him with fluttering excitement, like a groupie. And he was supposed to *work* with her? Whoever had come up with that idea? Feminists, he supposed.

He smiled. 'I am. You're cold?' She rolled her eyes. 'Take my portable heater,' he said. They both moved toward it and gently collided as they bent down. Giggling, Annette swayed on her heels and grasped his arm. 'You all right?' he said, putting a hand on her waist and letting it linger a moment. He'd never touched her before and noticed how she was thicker, and softer, than Lynne.

When she'd gone Dayton shut his door and looked at his hands, where his hands should be, remembering the feel of Annette's body and allowing some pornographic images to flit by until he started to get hard. He sat at his desk, ignoring the occasional telephone bleep or knock. The uninteresting files were pushed aside, the voice-mail messages deleted. A paperweight caught his eye: it was a polished glass orb with a kind of white explosion in the centre. Peering into it, Dayton saw a miniature office window, but no shadow of himself.

What did it all mean? The fear evoked by that question was gone. For he was discovering the meaning himself, wasn't he? An insight had come to him that first day of invisibility, when he was in the shower: *affliction* can be another word for *evolution*. He'd been through the pain. And now?

He felt clean. He felt new.

By nine-thirty Dayton had made up his mind and sketched a preliminary plan. He called Mr Ong's office. Though it was thirteen hours later in Tiajin, he was only slightly surprised when a secretary answered.

The hairstylist wanted to know what he was doing tonight.

'Celebrating.'

With a playful look, all raised eyebrows, she shifted to his right side. Dayton had been coming to her regularly and liked her. Everything she said and did was controlled, like she'd already read the script and nailed it.

'Sounds fun. What's the occasion?'

'Promotion.'

'Well, that's not surprising,' she said, making little sprays of hair as she trimmed above his ears.

It had been beautiful to watch John and Brad's faces as the news sank in, as Ong's voice, coming from a black phone mid-table in the boardroom, conveyed the new strategic plan and necessary HR adjustments to support it – 'to carry the company to a future of glorious success' was what Ong actually said, in a moment of Maoist overstatement. Quadrupled R&D budget. Major expansion. Revised management structure. Dayton had practically sprung down the street afterwards. By year-end there would be a corner suite with a view of the mountains for him, the new CEO, in addition to a delightful salary. He'd raced home, scooped up Lynne off the couch and carried her into the bedroom – something he'd always wanted but had never been motivated enough to do.

Dayton eyed the stylist's body. Her miniskirt had been stitched from an old sweatshirt; part of the word 'Roughriders' arced across her ass. As she moved her short top exposed a puckered, gold-ringed navel.

CEO was a solid start. But almost too easy, a mere one-handed twist of the future. Trend's new strategic plan, which had come to him with such visionary clarity and been adopted so readily, would soon become familiar. The scenery would get boring.

'That does it,' the stylist said, reaching for a large hand mirror to show Dayton what he couldn't see. He wondered whether she'd done a good job. Lynne would have to tell him. He ran his hand along his hairline, feigned satisfied engagement with the mirror. As he was paying they flirted again and he became bold. It was after six, only staff remained in the shop. Would she like to have a quick drink?

He brought the car around and, as he waited, took from his pocket a plastic toothpick wrapped in a silk eyeglass cloth, and carefully removed from his back teeth the remnants of an especially dry, chewy muffin he'd eaten earlier. He rinsed well with bottled water. Left a voice mail for Lynne. Then the stylist emerged, wearing a white fun-fur jacket. She looked like an exotic bird; her scent infused the car. 'Where would you like to go?' he asked. She shrugged, then suggested a place. She'd brought a CD. *I'd like to, I'd like to, I'd like to,* huffed a sleepy-sounding woman over a drum-machine beat that was like a hammer splitting ice. The steering wheel rotated with autopilot smoothness as they zoomed onto the Granville Street bridge, the gearshift seeming to move by pure will. With an efficient whir the sunroof opened and Dayton and his date lit cigarettes.

The stylist turned and looked him over. 'I love the way you dress,' she said.

'What about my hair? A very gorgeous woman did it.' He met her eyes. She was staring right back.

Traffic stopped suddenly. Waiting, they finished their cigarettes and listened to the music in an atmosphere that seemed to him poised on the verge of action. Dayton made some calculations: he'd been in the salon for an hour and this was his fifth or sixth visit to this woman, so that was about seven hours, plus the car ride. Women needed time to decide; was this enough? Traffic was still stopped. Dayton shifted to park. Leaning over, he placed his lips lightly on the stylist's cheek, drew back, felt her face turning, then fastened on two full lips sticky with gloss. The kiss was slow and deep, and they tongued each other until parted by an irritated honk.

Up ahead something was happening: cars were pulling over into the outside lane on both sides of the bridge. With stop-and-start progress they advanced until they could see an accident: two cars had collided. The front corner of one was crushed, and a person who seemed to be the driver was standing outside the open door holding his arm while several people, perhaps other passengers, huddled about him. The other car was in the inner lane on Dayton's side: he could see the jagged remains of the front windshield, the anguish on bystanders' faces. As they crept past the bent hood pebbled with glass he heard the stylist exclaim, was aware she was craning to see. Several metres in front, belly-down and askew on the road, lay the body of a man who was clearly dead. He wore sneakers and jeans. By his head a baseball cap lay upturned and plaintively empty, like a donation bowl.

Dayton stopped the car. The visible half of the man's young face was splattered with blood and viscous blobs, while under one cheek was a spreading pool. But the mouth compelled Dayton the most: open, the jaw had slouched to one side to reveal the lower teeth. A rill of blood trickled over and out.

Ignoring the stylist, who was shouting at him to keep going, Dayton got out and went over to the body. Someone had draped a jacket, possibly the victim's own, over the man's torso, but no one stood near him. Dayton felt like he was walking onto a stage. With a neat tuck of his trousers, conscious of the faces turned his way, he crouched before the man. The angle wasn't right. Lie down? Messy. Reaching into his pocket, Dayton removed and unwrapped the plastic toothpick, placed it against the man's lower teeth, and firmly pushed. The jaw gave a little more. Ah! This was what he'd wanted to see: the marvellous slick redness inside, tunnelling to black.

'Are you a doctor?' It was a middle-aged woman holding a cell phone.

Dayton stood, rewrapping the toothpick. 'No, just someone,' he said. *Someone not like you at all, thank God.* He giggled. He really couldn't help it, he felt so light, so lawless. How could he explain?

Devotion

Emily and Clive once went to a party held in honour of a dead cat. A memorial-fundraiser, actually, since kitty's exit had cost. The cat's owner, an actress Clive had met on set, greeted them at the door dressed in clinging black. In the cramped living room of an East Vancouver apartment, feline memorabilia were displayed like botanical specimens or works of art, while various objects such as small appliances or glassware were tagged. A group of mostly female guests sat on the floor. With their bottles of beer Emily and Clive edged along the living room's perimeter, nibbling nacho chips. They came to a colourful sign with an arrow pointing down: KITTY'S BOWL, it said. And there it was. 'Oh God, this is so Vancouver,' Emily whispered. A decade in Toronto had altered her perspective of her home city, and with Clive in tow she'd returned to find Vancouver lovely yet jejune, a not unpleasant reminder of her own acquired worldliness. Yet despite the incident of the Dead Pussy Party, as Clive called it, when their dog Lewis unexpectedly died, Emily also began to feel the need for something extraordinary.

Lewis's nails clicked across the hardwood floor. Drowsily, Emily woke from a deep sleep. A speckled shadow, the full moon through the chestnut tree outside, fluttered on one wall like a school of fish, softly chattering, it seemed. She sat up: there was another movement in the room – Lewis, pacing at the foot of their bed. The crown of his heavy head travelled down the length of the footboard, reversed and returned. *Lewis!* she whispered, but he didn't respond. 'What is it?' She slid out of bed and knelt before him but he wouldn't acknowledge her, and when she tried to take his face in her hands his head wagged and pulled away. His eyes were evasive; he whined. Emily woke Clive. But Lewis wouldn't be put on his leash, wouldn't stop his agitated – now clearly panicky – pacing, and soon collapsed with a long, surrendering sigh that took him to the floor. For a moment they were all still. Then Clive, squatting naked beside the dog, bent over him with a groan, and the flurry of futile rescue began.

They were in an emergency veterinarian's office. Lewis lay dead on the examining table. Under the fluorescent lights, with his canines jutting from parted jaws, he looked grim and beastly – a felled horror-show predator brought in for scrutiny by Emily and Clive, the hot young sleuths who'd solved the case. Death strips you, Emily thought. It takes away your image. You get a death-body, lurid and unlovable. But she refused to go along with Death. Though the room had no windows she was still very aware of the night outside, the marine dampness that she'd felt in the parking lot. Its silence. Though Clive and the vet had retreated from the table she remained at Lewis's side, her fingers scrunching and releasing his fur.

The vet was attempting to transition them from shock to practicalities, Emily realized after a moment. 'Why can't we just take him home and put him in the freezer?' she said.

Under her open jacket she was still wearing the tank top she slept in, a thin white garment through which her nipples were plainly visible. Clive raised his eyes and stared. He'd never seen her braless in public. She looked tatty and unstable. Sexy.

'I don't think we have room for him, babe,' he said, getting up to put his hands on her shoulders.

'Then we'll just have to buy one. A bigger freezer. Can Lewis stay here tonight?' Emily asked the vet, whose eyes darted anxiously toward Clive. 'You wouldn't mind that, would you?' Emily murmured, rubbing her nose against one of Lewis's ears. 'Such a good, good dog.'

A while later, after explanations of city bylaws and storage limitations, Emily and Clive were seated in the reception room holding hands and reviewing cremation forms. Clive kept rubbing his face. He'd worked a fourteen-hour shift building a film set for the third day in a row, had only a few hours' sleep, then hoisted his dying dog into the car. He felt compressed into a two-dimensional space that wanted him flat. Prone. 'This is so stupid,' said Emily, yanking the pen from his idle fingers. 'We can't even bury our own fucking dog. I thought the city was trying to become more environmentally friendly?' Her face was flushed. She'd become nasty with the vet earlier and still hadn't cried. She dated and signed the form and flipped it over. Underneath was a glossy brochure advertising animal-shaped cremation repositories made by a Vancouver craftsperson who supplied the clinic. *Eternal Pets: Preserving Your Cherished Memories.* There was much to choose from: breeds, poses, miniature to life sizes, materials. All manner of cats and cherubic kittens were available. There were dogs exuding wisdom and nobility, pert budgies, stoic turtles, hamsters forever running their treadmills – urns for pets. Emily turned the pages. Clive frowned.

'Ew,' he said.

Instinctively they both headed for the bedroom when they reached home, as if they could lie down and wake up again; instead they found what looked like a petty crime scene: tousled bedsheets, leash on the floor, a lamp knocked over when they were picking Lewis up. Clive slid off his jeans and flopped on the mattress still wearing his jacket. 'God, poor Lewis,' he said, his voice craggy. 'He seemed like such a healthy guy.'

Emily sat by the foot of the bed. In her lap lay the items they'd brought home from the veterinarian's: Lewis's collar and some tufts of his brindled hair in a zip-lock bag. In the car she'd absently rebuckled the collar at the usual spot, making a hollow ring. The ashes would be ready in two business days.

Why two?

Deep, rhythmic breathing came from Clive. 'Genetic,' Emily said, repeating the vet's diagnosis. Nothing to be done. Only three years ago they had chosen Lewis from among many eager dogs at the Humane Society. He'd been the most composed. She'd not wanted a dog, especially a hyper one. An animal in the house meant work and smells and noise. Steaming turds would be her lot. Hair would invade. Plus, her only intimate experience with a dog happened as a child with a creature so revolting she had never wanted to own one: Carlos, her grandmother's brown miniature poodle, was unfixed and so unappeasedly horny that even his own 'special pillow', deeply dented from his dedicated thrusts, didn't stop his attachment to any available leg. But Clive had argued. He'd been unusually focused, almost driven.

Emily fingered the baggie of hair. Fine swirls of brown, black and grey, even red, these little fibres contained in their inmost chambers the mysterious energy that had created Lewis, given him a butterfly-shaped stain on his tongue, his twitchy eyebrows. A cosmic experiment was Lewis – like everything else in the Petri-dish universe, except that something else always slipped in past the DNA. A painter would show it as two dots of light in the eyes, two dots for whatever it was that made Lewis look at them, as he lay on the examining table near the end, with an expression of sad apology.

Her hands were trembling. Lewis was dead and Lewis was exactly what she wanted right now for comfort. Lewis would not fall asleep in a crisis – he'd be right in there, excitedly giving her warning, protection or kisses, whatever was required. Almost 6:30 a.m., time for his morning walk. Emily mashed the baggie against her mouth, wishing she could swallow it, gag or suffocate the loss. As the sob started she bent double and locked her temples between her knees, squeezing as she cried and cried, squeezing until her head throbbed. Then all the energy spiralled down again and the black space snapped shut, leaving her limp. Crawling up the bed to Clive, she curled into his side and fell asleep with her face against his warm and musky groin.

'You *bought* one of those?'

Emily stared at the picture on her computer screen: sapling on a suburban lawn, out-of-focus home and garage in the background, blue sky. Hanging in midair over the sapling, a green watering can rained down. *We make your ideas grow,* the slogan said. The ad belonged to a company that made ceiling tiles, but could have been promoting a bank, a nursery, a consulting firm. Specificity decline, Emily called it. Strange how jumbled marketing had become in an age of specialization. An ad for men's underwear showed mountains, an ad for gasoline showed mountains, and so on. At least some bright person had convinced these tile people to redesign their visuals, which brought the ad to the small graphic design group Emily worked for. She picked up the latest home page layout she'd sketched: the number of moving parts was dizzying. The company wanted key information to appear on the screen 'like tiles', but 'not to be static'. 'Sliding tiles?' Emily had suggested. 'Floating tiles,' the company had said. She reread the slogan. The picture was a visual husk; it made her feel drained and weak.

Clive had come home and was in the living room. She knew what he was looking at.

Getting back to work hadn't been easy – it had been brutal. Clive didn't know, he was gone all day while she struggled to reinstate her routine without Lewis's loud yawns and snorts, his dream grunts and sudden scrambles to his feet – the creaturely noise that had given way to the buzz of refrigerator and computer. She'd opened all the windows to let in the wind, but with it came traffic. The hours spilled, her discipline got sloppy. Before they'd adopted Lewis, she used to call Clive sometimes four or five times a day. The phone was a fix – a connection, however tenuous, to a richer, preferable reality beyond clients and co-workers, even though for a long time their calls had been dwindling to mere information exchange. They would have conversations like –

'How was your morning?'

'They set a guy on fire.'

'Really?'

'Yeah, it was weird. They threw gasoline all over him and then lit it. I guess he was wearing this special suit underneath his clothes. Still, he was totally in flames. And there I was ten feet away, eating a muffin. How's your morning going?'

'I've been working on that bakery ad. They sent it back because they thought the picture of the bread didn't look fresh enough.'

'Unreal.'

Emily hated this, but attempts to shift direction by being more sharing and personal often felt forced, off key, and didn't work on the phone anyway. Intimacy doesn't come from words, or even from our desire for it, she concluded, regarding this thought as another signpost on the road to maturity.

That was one of the advantages of getting Lewis, Clive had said. Not improved phone conversations, but company. She'd also silently noted and felt the timing: seven years into their relationship, the apartment decorated, the horizon empty of events. The dog worked: she stopped calling Clive so frequently, not only stopped needing to, but wanting to. The walks with Lewis two or three times each day, out in the elements with nothing but motion required, were often her most calm and pleasurable moments. Home was enmeshed with work, which was growing more repetitive and less satisfying, and with Clive, about whom, yes, she could often say the same.

'Emily?'

She rose from her desk and slowly entered the living room.

'Is that what I think it is?' Clive said.

She nodded.

Against one wall stood an art deco cabinet they had bought when they were furnishing the apartment. Inside were mostly books and DVDs, but on top lay a few favourite pieces they'd picked up at art openings or on vacation: a piece of Astroturf-covered Styrofoam on which two tiny plastic men, naked, walked hand in hand toward an apple tree; a Jack-and-Jill salt and pepper set; a photo montage of someone taking photographs of himself in a mirror; a chunk of the Berlin Wall. All these had been displaced by a hefty ceramic sheepdog with shiny black eyes and a red, slightly vulgar-looking tongue sticking from its mouth. Emily scratched the back of her neck. She was not unaware that $249.95 ·for a funeral urn sheepdog (the closest breed resembling Lewis's Airedale/Mystery Parent mix) was a swindle along the lines of silverplated coffins, not quite as bad as a Dead Pussy Party, because it was a private gesture, but in some ways worse, since the urn increased the death bill and would stay with them as long as they could stand it.

'And is it ... filled?' Clive said.

'Look. When I went to the vet's office today they had him in this cardboard box tied with white ribbon that they handed me across the counter. It was like they were giving me a present.' Emily's voice wavered and she swallowed. Clive, who fell asleep in a crisis, was not to see her cry now. 'And I thought this would be better – better than a box, at least,' she said.

'Oh Jimmy,' he said with a smile, and hugged her. It was one of his oldest names for her, going back to an early blunder, when in a moment of high intimacy he'd somehow garbled 'Emily'. The name gave her a strange feeling now; it was like an old scent from a long unopened drawer.

Clive picked up the dog and examined it. Shallow grooves ran along the material to suggest hair. 'God, this is pretty bad. Couldn't we just get an ordinary urn? Or a nice wooden box?'

'Clive, you weren't the one who had to go there.'

'I know, babe, but I'm ...' His head dipped. He stepped back from the cabinet with a resigned 'Okay, whatever.'

Emily centred Lewis, as she already thought of the urn. She could buy a piece of cloth to lay underneath, perhaps velvet or silk. It was on the bus to the emergency vet clinic, angry at Clive for his seemingly agile shouldering of the loss while she had been almost immobilized, that she'd remembered the urn brochure they'd been given the night of Lewis's death. The figurines had seemed amateurish and goofy then, yet familiar. Where from? At first she thought it must be an ad she'd looked at, one among the thousands. But when the memory surfaced it was more eerie and foreign, an image from her days in Toronto: a glass case in the Egyptian collection at the Royal Ontario Museum. Inside were two animal sarcophagi from tombs, holding tiny bodies of cats that had been mummified along with their masters and laid in coffins painted with the same Egyptian eyes, staring from feline faces. And that was what she wanted even before she saw the ribboned box: a container for Lewis's essence, a death body as dignified and lovely as him. At the clinic she'd purchased the urn and then at home sat on the living-room floor and carefully poured in the grey grains and sealed them. She brought the dog onto her lap; its solidity was like pressure on a swelling. The grief began contracting to a sharp, concentrated hurt.

Clive returned from the shower wearing a towel, the heat from his skin touching her as he stood close behind. 'Are you going to bed?' she asked, turning her head.

'Yeah,' he said, his eyes looking into hers. Deep, precise lines arced from the corners of his eyes to his cheekbones. Age was making him elegant, more like the fine arts grad he was, even as that life receded. The strongest remnant of it surfaced in these moments, after work, when no matter how hard the day had been he would voice the same question. Household chores or a conversation of any length would soon make Clive frown and sigh, but for long and generous lovemaking he had a subterranean reserve of energy that she found baffling, enviable, thrilling or repulsive, depending on her mood. What never changed was the question/answer prelude and her awkward role as the less predictable character who determined the action.

She kissed him quickly on the cheek. 'Good night.'

Alone, she lay on the couch across from the cabinet. Whatever frustration Clive might be feeling, guilt-motivated sex would be a tainted and sorrowful offering, the honest flame between them grown too flickering and fragile to choke further.

Emily's eyes fluttered closed. As she fell asleep she saw herself on her back, like one of the little sarcophagi in cradled repose, her skyward eyes serene as she floated through the night, drifting like a queenly canoe toward heaven.

On the video screen a cartoon uterus was being infiltrated by tadpole sperm.

'When was that?' Clive was saying.

'Last summer in New York.'

Clive grinned. 'That's brilliant.'

The woman mouthed something else Emily couldn't hear over the music. Did Clive think this woman was brilliant? The music was insanely loud. Why the hell did it have to be this loud? An electronic drum beat into her body. And this mechanical pummelling was supposed to make people relax.

'What's your role in the film?' she asked a young woman who'd been standing quietly beside her. The woman, who did wardrobe, had spiky red hair and wore large, black-rimmed glasses, a tartan miniskirt, and a pink T-shirt with an anime schoolgirl staring out from it. It seemed as though an entire generation lay between them, Emily thought, aware of her own attractive but comparatively boring black dress.

The woman sucked on an ice cube as she answered Emily's questions. 'So far the shoot's been okay. There's nothing, like, challenging about the clothes or anything, just the egos.'

'Like who?'

'Well, *he's* the worst,' she said, raising an index finger from her tumbler to indicate an area next to the martini bar. Although the actor was hidden in the crowd, they both knew he was there. Everyone felt the gravitational pull of the few film stars scattered throughout the quadrants of the party; the guests' eyes shone brighter, and bodies betrayed their affected nonchalance by angling toward specific locations. 'He's like, totally picky,' the wardrobe woman said. 'Unlike Heather. Heather's amazing.' They glanced toward another quadrant.

'Cool,' Emily said. Every few minutes the overhead lights changed colour, casting faces into alternating shades of red, yellow, blue. Whenever the blue lights came on a disco ball would start spinning, filling the room with swirling blue bubbles. Bubbles rose on legs and chests. Moonlit faces floated by. The woman Clive was talking to had put her hand on his arm and leaned toward him, her dress revealing more and firmer cleavage than Emily's. Clive's eyes did not drift down. Yes, but he knows I'm watching, she thought.

'I'll take you some time,' the wardrobe woman was saying. 'We can do a whole day spa. It's amazing. You'll love it. You work at home, right?'

'Right. That would be great.'

'I can't wait to be at home,' she said sadly. 'I haven't been there except to sleep in like five months. Isn't that insane?'

Emily's eyes drifted to the video screen, on which a black-and-white film showed a 1950s-style family relaxing in their living room. Mother knitted smilingly. Father concentrated on his paper. Young lad lay on the floor with a comic book. Then the cartoon uterus came on again. So it was an old sex ed film – ho ho. Was this mockery supposed to be titillating? Clever? Or maybe just whimsical, randomness this season's sophistication.

Emily turned to talk to the wardrobe woman, but she'd gone. Now it was her turn to stand quietly. Regardless of what she knew about the day-to-day grind of film shoots, going to Clive's work parties always made her doubtful. Partly it was the extreme hype that film generated, its narcissistic need for attention. There was also the dull ring of saying *I work at home*. Now there's a line with zero glamour. Yet what irritated her more was probably just the simple truth that this was the world she and Clive had chosen. They used to talk bigger – about doing interesting, socially meaningful work, about having children. How they had become unconvinced, whether the source of the problem lay in one or both of them or perhaps somewhere else, an environmental compound of influences – Emily didn't know. Maybe the real problem was their need to be convinced.

When Gregor came for the first time after Lewis died, he gave Emily a tight hug at the door. 'I'm so sorry I wasn't here sooner,' he murmured into her ear with other sweet condolences, embracing her so long that they actually took some breaths in unison; she could feel the gentle, gill-like opening and closing of his ribs, the rise of his chest against hers. She slid a hand down his back, stopping at the waist of the jeans that arousal was urging her to move beneath. Reg, Gregor's black terrier, scampered around the apartment sniffing, finally letting out a sharp bark.

'Yes, Reg, your friend is gone!' said Gregor, letting go of Emily and sitting the couch. 'It's so –'

He stared.

'What is that?'

'It's uh, it's a kind of memorial,' she said, quickly heading to the kitchen to make coffee. The morning after the film party she'd woken up missing Lewis like water, like sun. She'd moved the art deco cabinet, replacing it with a low wooden table, in the centre of which the sheepdog now erectly sat. Around him was a kind of garden of smooth river stones, sprigs of fresh lavender, baby's breath and dried moss. Coloured glass containers held tea light candles. A framed photograph of Lewis was accessorized by his collar.

'Why a sheepdog, exactly?' Gregor said, and Emily explained about the urn brochure. He shook his head. 'Wow. I wish I'd known about those when Angus died.' Gregor's previous dog, Angus, had also been a black terrier. Before him in line there had been another: Gus.

Gregor, gay and gorgeous, had eyes the perfect colour for tears. When these brimmed, as they did now, they intensified a limpid quality that seemed his essence. He had a chaste smile and Emily always thought he would look natural posed against a hedge with water gently sluicing his limbs. At forty-one he appeared about thirty, a problem he was trying to solve by growing a goatee. He reached over and held Emily's hand. They drank their coffee while Reg settled down to gnaw on an old bone of Lewis's. Why is love so much easier with this man? Emily wondered.

When Gregor and Reg dropped by a few days later, the bone was on the memorial table along with a second photograph and fresh flowers. There was also a china bowl in which a mat of dog hair (culled from Lewis's brush, never the zip-lock bag) lay on a bed of pebbles. Every morning Emily refreshed the flowers and lit the candles. The scratch and hiss of the match and its musky whiff of sulphur, or the orange tint in the ceramic revealed by a rooty-smelling marigold – these small experiences had a density that reassured, for a while.

Emily and Gregor lay on the couch at opposite ends with their arms draped over each other's legs. Gregor grinned. 'Ask me how my foray into Internet dating is going.' Emily asked. 'It's … yielding interesting results,' he said. Gregor often spoke with a pseudo-scientific manner that he was quite aware of, perhaps playing the psychiatrist he was studying to be. Normally she found it funny, but not today.

'Tell on,' she said.

'Well, there's been a rather strange incident involving an engineering consultant with a penchant for leather.' Emily's eyes widened. The story, as Gregor related it, was that a man he'd met online invited him over for a very nice lunch, then showed him 'an entire store's worth' of leather clothes inside a custom-made closet in the bedroom. The man outfitted Gregor and himself, and then –

'You allowed this?' Emily said.

'Oh yes.'

'And he wore the same thing?'

'Totally.'

Emily's fingers lightly tapped the shin that was under her hand. She detested this wealthy pervert, this aging Batman who turned Gregor into a Robin catamite. Gregor was supposed to be a gentle fountain boy, good as gold. She listened reluctantly, vaguely embarrassed and unsure how to respond.

'So, was it good?' she said.

He gave her that Mona Lisa smile. 'It was certainly interesting. It's hard to move when you're wearing leather, you know. You can't even really *feel* anything through it.'

'Ah.'

In a little while Gregor picked up Reg, saying he needed to go home and tend his wounds. 'A joke,' he added with a grin, then pinched her cheek.

Emily returned to her desk to stare at the revised ceiling tile ads that had arrived by courier or this morning. An itchy irritability that began with Gregor's arrival had turned into a full-on foul mood. No, not a mood, a taste. Disgust. The computer, a whiny plastic box with an unpleasant glare: her work tool. Work: exhausted symbols reassembled as style. Herself: an ensemble of dissatisfactions and petty lust.

When they first got Lewis, he'd been a pain. She'd be working and he'd come sit beside her desk just to watch her, spellbound. He'd follow her to the kitchen. The bathroom. If she was reading he would sit directly in front of her with attentive eyes. 'For God's sake, what is it?' she'd snap. Lewis's eyebrows twitched. If she sounded really angry he would make this gulping sound and lie down. It was pathetic. However, one day as she was stretching out on her back the dog lay down beside her. When she'd turned her head to him, he'd groaned softly and licked her chin. His eyes were black and wet. A word came to her: devotion. Here it was, this was what it looked like.

She called Clive.

'Can we talk?'

'__ aser Valley ____ highway. Coquitlam?'

'What for?' (Laughter.) 'Who's that?'

'We're driving out to __ teamster ____?'

'What?'

'Can you hear what I'm saying?'

She hung up. During the next hour she stood at various windows looking out. The phone rang. She turned it off and shut down the computer. In the living room she sat cross-legged on the floor and tried to meditate for the second or third time in her life. Clear the mind, she thought. Go to nothing. Thoughts pushed in and were shoved back; in a while they became more floaty, an observable stream, and then abruptly she felt like she was dropping, dropping through a borderless black space. Her eyes popped open. Her legs ached. Standing up, she shook each one and started walking around the room in a circle that gradually shrank to a line paced in front of the memorial, back and forth.

Clive's footsteps woke her.

'Holy shit, Emily, what have you been doing?' She sat up on the couch, groggily registering the hallway light and dim form of Clive, still in his fleece jacket and dusty jeans, looking tired but capable of something more. He flicked on the overhead lights.

'Christ!'

From the centre of the memorial table, the sheepdog, now wearing the collar, rose from a makeshift wooden pedestal like a small deity issuing from and presiding over the fecundity below. Daffodils, black-eyed Susans, and other bright flowers filled most of the table. There was even a little bowl of water with floating petals. 'What you do, enlarge it every day? It looks like an altar.'

Emily straightened her blouse and hair. 'I don't see anything wrong with it.'

'It's huge and weird. Even the urn itself without all this other whatever-it-is. A Buddhist garden? I mean, I didn't say anything at first –'

'Oh yes you did. You said it was tacky.'

'Well, it is tacky. It looks ridiculous. I mean, think about it. You don't put a human being's ashes into a human-shaped urn.'

'The Egyptians did it. They even did it with their animals too.'

Clive ran his hand through his hair. It was late in the day; the synapses weren't firing easily. 'Yes,' he said slowly, 'but that was different. First of all, it was *burial*. Second, it was part of a whole religion. They buried people with their possessions, with money, because the idea was that people needed these things in the afterlife. They even buried them with slaves sometimes.'

'Well I'm burying Lewis that way too,' Emily said, her voice rising.

'That doesn't make sense.'

'I don't care.' She started to walk toward her study, but Clive intervened and gripped her arm. So rarely did he get angry that it frightened her when it happened.

'You don't even act like you love me,' he said. Emily gave a shocked laugh and tried to pull away, but he stepped with her, bringing his face in close. 'It's like you love our dog – our *dead* dog – more than me. I'm just this boring guy who comes home from work.'

'You're jealous of the fucking dog,' Emily said, attempting an ironic smile.

'You never touch me. And even when we're making love, it's like you're somewhere else now. You never initiate it anymore.'

'How can I? There's never any space to initiate anything.'

The hurt on his face was plain, but she refused to take responsibility for it. 'You're the one who wanted me to have a dog. You're the one who wanted me to like him.'

'Like. Love. Yes, but stay in reality. It's like you don't even see me anymore. If you're sad, talk to me.'

'It's not that easy.'

'And it's easier to – what? Communicate with that? *Commune* with it?' He let her go. 'I don't understand what you get from it.'.

A white petal lay on the floor and she picked it up, smoothing it between her finger and thumb. The petal curled into a roll, then a tight twist that she pressed into her palm. 'Pure love,' she said quietly.

Clive turned away with a sigh.

He was awake when she came to bed much later, on his back looking up at the ceiling. In the same position Emily lay down in her tank top and boxer briefs and waited for a motion or word.

'Lewis was perfect,' she said.

'He was what he was.'

She looked out the window. The moon was waning; only a thin bright crescent hung in the sky.

'I just want there to be some place clean,' she said after a while.

Clive rolled over. 'I know one,' he whispered. His hand touched her, sliding over her chest and belly and under the elastic of her shorts, slipping between her legs. Carefully, his index finger found her opening and moved inside. She put her arm around him and he settled his face against her neck. In minutes he was asleep.

He was wrong about her and Lewis, Emily thought. There was no communion because she didn't believe the dog had a soul. Not him, not herself, not anyone. Nice idea but untrue: the sky just reached up up up until things went black forever and there was no sacred canopy, no Throne of God listening to life below. Lewis's love wasn't part of a system. Yet it had happened, primitively and perfectly, and now she wanted that soul to pray for, to pray for her.

Emily shifted her legs. Clive's hand dropped down to her thigh. She lay listening to his breathing. Barely visible now, a speckled shadow moved back and forth across one wall, like a school of fish.

In the Woods

Cal sat at a corner table in the lodge's dining room. For the first time on the trip he was alone, and not just for breakfast. His wife lay ill in their room, and an entire day on his own in this town waited for him like a stiff wheel to be turned and turned. Naksup. The aspiring resort's attractions were advertised on its web site as 'Big Waters, Big Mountains, Big Smiles'. With deliberate slowness, Cal spread the rest of the patted butter and jam onto his toast and finished it.

A teenage waiter removed Cal's plate. Breakfast was officially over, the guests departing. 'I want to verify your room service hours,' Cal said. 'My wife's not feeling well now, but she'll definitely want to order something later.' The waiter assured him that the kitchen would be open. He did not offer Cal a big smile, nor his good wishes for Ruth's recovery.

Cal glanced about the emptying room, hoping to snag a sympathetic eye or inviting smile from a departing guest. He picked up his coffee and signalled the waiter, who returned to pour a refill. 'Thanks!' Cal said warmly. He had an open, playful countenance that people usually responded to. Students liked him. Strangers would stop him for directions.

'We live in Vancouver, but I've never been up to the Kootenays,' he said. 'Felt it was time to see more of the province. We went over to Banff and Jasper last week, saw the ice fields. Incredible country up here. I was reading about your hot springs, how they form. I didn't realize that they're actually replenished by the snowfall each winter.' He chuckled, delighted to be dispensing knowledge.

The waiter grinned. 'Yeah,' he said, 'in the winter they're amazing, when all the snow's around.'

'I know what you mean,' said Cal. 'We were down at a resort in Colorado once in the winter, where they had an outdoor swimming pool. My wife tried it. She thought it was terrific.' He switched to a more confidential tone. 'Yes, it's really unfortunate that she's under the weather today. We came here especially so she could try the hot spring.' He grimaced. 'Arthritis. In the hips and knees. Very painful. And now,' he said, throwing up a hand in defeat, 'she can't even try the springs because she has a headache!'

The waiter, who'd been mechanically nodding, brightened. 'Oh, well, if you want to see something less commercial, there's a actually a nicer spring that people in town use, up the highway in the woods. I was just telling those guests at the next table about it. I think they're heading up.'

It irritated Cal that the boy said nothing about Ruth, but he asked about the springs anyway. The guests at the next table had been yachters, Americans with sunburnt noses who'd talked about the lakes, and he was curious to know what they were doing today. He got out his Naksup map and had the waiter jot down directions that he looked over, asking questions until he understood the way perfectly.

After finishing his coffee, Cal rose and thumbed the waist of his chinos a little lower on his belly. He strolled into the lobby and stood peering through the glass front doors at the parking lot. Here it was again: the uncomfortable sense of things being askew. It had pestered him throughout the trip, making him fret about schedules, sleep fitfully. Now, in solitude, the problem was obvious: it was his father's letter, of course.

A young couple were getting into their SUV. Cal pictured Ruth, lying upstairs with the curtains closed, one arm crooked over her brow as if to ward off the assault of pain. Earlier he'd sat by her hip and put soft questions to her pinched nostrils until she snapped at him to go and to stay gone; the migraine could linger into tomorrow if she didn't rest. Well, perhaps he'd check on their daughter then, and the dog. He went to the front desk and waited for a staff person to appear, then asked to use the phone. Cal's sister didn't answer, so he left a message. Then he chatted with the woman behind the counter until another guest arrived. Finally, at 11 a.m., he went out to the parking lot and unlocked the car.

The letter had arrived shortly before he and Ruth left home, and the weight, shape and feel of it in his hands had at first impressed Cal with a kind of awe. A letter! From his father! He couldn't remember ever receiving one before. A birthday card, sometimes. Mostly the letter talked about the 'retirement' cabin that Calvin Sr was building for himself on northern Vancouver Island. *So he can get even further away from people,* Cal had thought when he'd heard about the project at Christmas. His father wrote about the plans for the cabin's rooms and outlying buildings, the mechanisms that would supply self-sufficient power and recycle the water, all of which he'd designed himself. The plans seemed realistic; Calvin Sr was a talented builder, and at seventy-six still remarkably fit and independent. Yet near the end of the letter, his father had done something even more surprising than writing: he'd invited Cal up to the cabin, without any other family members, without even Ruth. 'It would be good to be alone, just the two of us for a change,' he'd written.

'The two of us'?

For a change?

The letter seemed to be groping toward a past that had barely existed, a few years of scattered father-son visits after the divorce when Cal was still a boy. Then Calvin Sr had moved away until the eighties, and for the last twenty or so years, ever since his father had returned to British Columbia and been peripherally reinstated in the family, Cal had with few exceptions seen him only at two annual family events: Mother's birthday party and Christmas Day dinner. The man was always dressed in a suit, which, together with the somewhat formal tone of these days, created a segregation everyone seemed happy with.

Cal pictured a building made of logs surrounded by impenetrable woods. An open-plan living area where interaction between father and son would occur. What kind of clothes did his father wear at home? Did he own a stereo? Flatware? He couldn't imagine conversation being sustained beyond the first quarter hour. An hour would be tough. And a day? The screen went blank, overwhelmed by lack of information.

Big waters, big mountains, big smiles.... Naksup had a lake, a downtown strip called Broadway that was about five minutes away and as many seconds long. He and Ruth had seen it yesterday when they arrived, but now Cal drove down it again, the late-spring morning revealing a sparse population of retirees and skateboarding teens, offers of T-shirts, tackle 'n' bait, local watercolours and Native crafts … not even a movie theatre and certainly not a bar open this early. He found a Chinese-Canadian diner with a grill cook as grim as a frontier cowboy. At one rear table, a bulky, ill-defined customer hunched over a crossword. Cal read his newspaper and an issue of *Discover* that he'd purchased at a convenience store. He ate a slice of cherry pie and a Panhandler's Triple Gold Sandwich (turkey breast, fried onion, mayo) washed down with a beer. He'd made it to two o'clock. Broadway again: distant birds wheeling near the mountains, herds of greybellied clouds. Cal swung into a parking lot by the pier and drummed his fingers on the sideview mirror. A cool wind was curling dark waves across the lake. Naksup's web site had also spoken of bygone industry: steamers that travelled the lake chain in the days before the railways and roads, ferrying gold-rush settlers, Slocan miners, trappers taking booty to Revelstoke. Yet we're a town of the future, the site boasted, positioning Naksup as an ideal retirement community, a year-round pleasure-seekers' paradise. The Tourist Information Booth was done up like a paddle-wheeler, the Seniors' Community Hall a log cabin. The web site showed smiling hikers, skiers, girls in bathing suits, a fisherman hoisting his stunned catch. And the natural Naksup Hot Springs, it assured, had been fully developed for visitor comfort.

Pathetic, Cal thought, regarding the deserted pier, the lonely lake. These interior towns – what were they but stopovers? You couldn't *holiday* here, it was like staying in Nanaimo or Tsawwassen. In his opinion, civilization in British Columbia consisted of Vancouver. Reading about places like Naksup was one thing; the local history, the geology – these, distilled and elucidated in good prose, engaged him. But for experience, his preferred vacation was a high-end package tour. Forget big mountains, how about some big cities, decadent cuisine, and the dynamic, dependable camaraderie of other vacationing couples, like this was part of the service. Ruth, however, had read about the hot springs and the relief they could bring for arthritis. Given her general state these days, the pains and prescriptions multiplying with age and the two of them barely past fifty, Cal had been more than willing to come.

Those yachters, though, they might provide good company. Cal's bathing suit and towel were in the car, along with the refreshments packed by Ruth. He examined his map: not far up the road to Revelstoke was the waiter's asterisk for the woodland spring and his scrawled directions. 'A thirty-minute drive,' Cal said aloud. 'I could do that. Check it out, come back and see the touristy ones too.' He was about to continue talking when a person emerged from a garage across the road. Cal's thoughts reverted to the waiter. Bit of a character, physically. He'd have to tell Ruth about him. 'Hoop earrings in *both* ears,' he muttered, starting the car.

The highway climbed away from town into the mountains. Cal switched on the radio, vainly searching for a news channel. He settled for tepid pop songs that failed to hold his interest and was soon brooding about his father's letter again. Why now? It was bizarre, and not in a way Cal had come to expect from his father, a man who was less parent than eccentric uncle, accepted or at least tolerated as a familiar oddity. Wanting to live in the wilderness like some pioneer! What was that – a kind of macho rebellion against age? In youth he'd been in the navy, emigrated. Ran around with women and ruined his marriage, then lived life alone, working, working. He was effective, had an impressive career engineering mines in North America, but to Cal his father never belonged. The Old World clung to him, a foreignness more subtle than his Rhineland accent, which still lingered after half a century in Canada. How he eventually got reinstated into the family, if only twice a year, still wasn't clear. His mother and sister arranged it, a gesture of forgiveness or even pity, perhaps, since his father had no one else.

Cal recalled last Christmas. His father hadn't acted any differently, he felt sure. As usual Calvin Sr had arrived punctually in his neat tweed suit, silver hair and moustache trimmed, shoes burnished. He'd greeted everyone individually once, distributed tasteful, semi-extravagant gifts to his grandchildren, and, with an almost reverent politeness, a beautifully wrapped gift to Cal's mother. 'And also we thank *you*, bird, for your honourable sacrifice,' he'd quipped at the end of grace. After dinner he'd retired to an armchair and remained there for the rest of the evening, like a portrait of himself.

Ruth had acknowledged the peculiarity of the letter's invitation, but had also called it 'lovely'. She wasn't offended at being excluded. 'Yes, well you won't be the one bored to death,' Cal said aloud as he drove toward the springs. 'Right. Enough of that.' He became cheerful. 'We need to keep a lookout for the highway sign that says – there it is!'

Cal braked and swung onto a narrow dirt road. Pleased to be so well prepared, he switched the vehicle into four-wheel drive and went bouncing up a rough, steep slope, stones pinging off the chassis. Gravity pulled him back and the shocks rebounded like bedsprings. 'Good God,' he said, as slender new branches bent and scratched against the windows. But the car handled well and his heart beat with excitement.

'A long ways in,' he said minutes later, squinting to see some end to the road. He imagined Ruth with him, witnessing his wild ascent. But no, not Ruth – the department's administrative secretary. With her long red hair and snug, tailored skirt. 'Better hope no one comes speeding down,' he told her, with a wrench of the gearshift. He flicked on the headlights. The road plateaued, veered, then began climbing the mountain again.

After some minutes the grade relaxed. Cal sighted a small dirt parking area marked with a sign, but not the hoped-for vehicles of others. The place was empty. A path led into the woods, where languorous steam obscured trees. Cal backed in and switched off the engine. As he stepped outside, the cold hit him. He exhaled an ethereal plume. Down below the days were hovering in the mid-teens and Ruth had left the heater on in the car, but since leaving town he'd climbed much higher, his cotton shirt and pants unsuited to the new climate. He strolled to the edge of the path: the ground was moist, and within a tire rut lay a fragile floor of ice.

'Good lord,' Cal gasped, but quietly. The car engine tapped. A bird darted. Hearing a burble of water, he followed the short path into the woods to find not one but several rock-lined pools encircled by narrow wooden platforms. Sluiceways linked the steamiest pool, which seemed the source, to the others. With a grunt and a creaking of joints, he squatted down to test the temperature: hot, but bearable. The mildly sulphurous water had a pleasing, slightly oily feel.

Cal looked back at the car, glad of its presence. He wasn't a woodsy man, never had been, and bathing itself didn't attract him. Yet having come all this way, he felt obliged to linger. He rapped the platform, noting the fine handiwork, the planks' snug fit. 'Well done,' he commented to the anonymous builder who materialized by his side.

Returning to the car, he rummaged some cookies from the bag of snacks and ate them standing in a patch of sun as he gazed up the road, which burrowed on through the forest into a bright haze. The woods were spacious, with little underbrush; trees stretched away, illuminated by occasional sunbeams. He was exposed here yet reassured by the visibility: nothing would leap out at him. And if townspeople visited the spot then it must be reasonably safe. It was quite beautiful, really. Bird twitter, tree repose, scent of bark and needle. Ruth would have loved it. He saw her soaking in the pool, toasting him with a gin and tonic. They could have had a festive little day here.

That's it: a gin and tonic. A drink and a quick bathe, then drive back and tell Ruth. She wouldn't mind a checking-up on by then, surely.

Cal took the tonic and slippery green bottle of Tanqueray out of the cooler, got a lime and pint-sized plastic glasses from the snack bag. The cocktail fizzed cheerful juniper. Thinking a snack might be nice, he carried the cooler and other food to the platform and returned to the car. Then, stoled with his towel, he swayed down the path wearing his swimming trunks and shoes.

Settling on the platform, he eased his pallid, goose-pimpled legs into the water. His stomach slumped over the suit's waistband. It began much higher up than it used to, just below the round little breasts he'd grown. After the radical gains and losses of his thirties he'd paid diminishing attention to his body, which clearly had its own powerful agenda, so he was a little relieved not to be with a group of athletic strangers. When his legs felt comfortable, he slipped in and plopped down with a yelp. Soon he was enjoying the invigorating clap of cold air against his hot, sweaty skin. So this was how people could spend hours here! He sipped the drink, which was perfection. Water rippled across the pool, inching the waterline up and down the rocks. Cal took another drink and looked around at the woods: cedars, and other evergreens whose names he didn't know; lichen and moss, some ferns, tendrils with sanguine berries … funny how he'd learned so much about the world, yet growing things remained mysteries.

'But we don't live in the forests any more, so it makes sense,' he blurted. 'Humans adapt to their environments. If we lived here, we'd learn the berries and leaves like street signs.'

He took a gulp of gin. His nostrils flared. The alchemy of alcohol, heat, and cold mountain air was purging grit and grime that he didn't know were there. His body thrummed with a new energy; had he thought about it, he hadn't felt this vital since the last distant time he and Ruth made enthusiastic love. Those plants? He'd learn all about them – his next project! With a loud, grunting sigh he pushed off from the platform and paddled about.

What if he went and got Ruth? A bathe would probably cure her headache. 'Bathing – it's underrated in our society,' he told her, forgetting that the trip to the springs had been her idea. 'It has an ancient history in many cultures, you know. The Slavs, the Aboriginals of North America. The Romans, for example – do you know the city of Bath in England?' Ruth had changed into the breakfast waiter, his young, absorptive eyes fixed on Cal.

'The hot springs built by the Romans are still there and still hot. Ruth and I visited in '85. The whole complex is below street level now, but there's a central *impluvium* open to the sky. I assume you didn't study Latin in school? Well, in the atrium of a wealthy Roman home, the *impluvium* –'

A bird screeched. Cal cringed and looked around. For a moment, he was deeply embarrassed.

He swirled his drink and finished it. Over the years there'd been discoveries of his talking-aloud habit, by Ruth of course, and some incidents at the college that he'd been able to cover up. Once, however, a fellow teacher from work had spotted him on the street and pulled over to ask if he was all right. Cal hadn't realized he'd been moving his lips. Frightened and irritated, he'd jovially tried to dismiss his behaviour, but then the woman asked if Cal *heard voices*. And he realized the danger. Afterwards, he'd learned to automatically control his lips so he could carry on dialogues in his head, speaking aloud only when certain of solitude. Which he was: nothing out here but trees, which were getting less alien and disturbing through the dependable assistance of gin. He dragged the cooler toward himself and refreshed his drink, got out a bag of bagels and some sliced cheese. Poolside service, like some Club Med. A serving girl would be nice ... a Japanese. They were lovely, delicate creatures, those Japanese women.

Lounging against the platform drink in hand, Cal nodded, his upper body rocking as the urge to soliloquize grew. 'Question is,' he said to the waiter, 'will characteristic racial features disappear before too long? The mingling of peoples is already diluting distinctions. I read about a study predicting that in fifty years there will no longer be any natural blonds in the world. Even if our global diaspora didn't exist, urbanization would have an effect. The Asiatic eye, for example: that's made for wind and dust, labouring in the fields, isn't it? You don't need that on a commuter train.' Cal belched. 'Or perhaps we *will*, with the pollution in our cities. Who knows what we're developing right now?'

Satisfied with this conclusion, he pushed off again and, propelling his arms, brought his legs out in front of him and watched his steamy toes pop up. Then he drifted about the pool. His body felt supple and boyish, sexy even – the years, the extra weight, borne away on the water. Oh Fountain of Youth ... who knew if springs like these were not the origin of myth? He'd leave in a minute. For now he lay

back, floating, and his eyes fluttered closed against the slowly
whirling sky.

Waking took effort. The spring's soporific trickling gently tickled his
ears. Opening his eyes, Cal felt jabbing pain in his neck and a sickly
weakness everywhere else. Something touched his arm and he flailed.
The plastic cup floated away.

He sat up in a panic. The light had dimmed. He remembered
how he'd felt sleepy and, sitting comfortably on a boulder in the shal-
lower section of the pool, the water just above his belly, he'd folded
his towel and put his head down for a moment on the platform. Slept,
unfortunately. The crick in his neck hurt. But he was otherwise fine,
except it was past sundown and he was rather drunk or dehydrated or
both. There was the cooler, which he'd stupidly left open. And the car,
glowing at the end of the path.

Glowing?

He cursed.

With shaking arms he heaved himself out. Ah: cold air. But still
too much gin inside. Wrapping himself in the towel, he lurched up
the path. The car's headlights shone weakly.

Cal switched off the lights, waited, then tried the engine. It made
a grinding noise. But the battery couldn't be dead already! He tried
again. 'Come on,' he said, coach to the flagging athlete. 'You've got
loads of energy. Just turn over, that's it, turn over ...'

He slumped back, exhausted. 'Okay. We won't flood the engine.
It must just be the cold.'

'No it's not,' Ruth said.

Cal peered up at the sloe-coloured sky and ragged black line of the
forest canopy. Visibility had dwindled to a small vicinity in which only
the closest trees were distinct; all else was gloom. Motionless, Cal
waited. Nothing chirped or fluttered any more. A hushed finality lay
over the mountain, the lying down of the day. Soon night would
awake, and with it other things that he well remembered from childhood camping trips, the awful sounds that were audible only after his
parents and sister were inside the trailer, and the fire burnt out, and

his brother wheezing by his side in the tent: indefinable rustlings and thumps, strange cries, the hideous snap of a branch in the dark.

That's enough – get a plan. First, he needed to drink lots of water and get dressed before he caught a chill. He kept a pencil flashlight in the glove compartment – and the emergency cell phone! Preparedness once again. Cal grabbed them and slid out of the car dizzily.

Once opened, the phone emitted a promising blue glow and little digital squares began roving up and down its screen. Though he hated not having the car at his back, Cal walked into the middle of the road. Waited. Finally, the squares were replaced by a message: OUT OF RANGE.

Okay.

Don't panic.

Technology is finicky, upset by the unfamiliar. The car and the phone might require time to orient. Cal got dressed and rehydrated, then set about retrieving his things from the spring, berating himself for leaving out the food – he could have been mauled in his sleep. He stored everything neatly away and methodically wrung out his trunks so as to prolong the moment when he got back in the car and retried the engine.

It went click.

Stunned moments passed. He told himself the car still might start, the phone find its signal. He would wait half an hour. He had a watch. It had a little button to illuminate it in the dark; that was lucky. He would wait half an hour and try again, and then he would ... he would not think about then.

The pool of visibility around the car was almost gone, the lowest branches of the nearest tree barely discernable. It would be a black night, a helpless, blind, country darkness. Its time had come.

Cal clutched the flashlight. Then he locked the doors.

The gin wore off. The cold got into him.

The plastic bags he'd tied over his shoes crinkled. His hands were buried in his groin for warmth. Though he'd drunk all the bottled water, plus the tonic, and had eaten a supper of bagels and cheese, potato chips, apples and fudge cookies, he felt empty and ill. How cold would it get? Ruth must be frantic! Shivering, he sat wrapped in the dog-haired afghan, more like a shawl, that normally Winston lay on for car trips. Winston himself, though only a spaniel, would have been a welcome companion now. The car was dark as a closet.

Thirty-minute increments.

Can a bear break a window? Bears weighed hundreds of pounds and their strength was, well, *bearish*. Which meant a hell of a lot. Cal imagined a bear shaking the car, rattling him senseless, then ripping the door off. He imagined it sniffing the wind for fudge cookies.

Perhaps a woodsy person would think of something else to do, but Cal couldn't figure out what. Hike to the highway? Too far and too risky with a tiny flashlight that could wink out any second. Two hours had passed and he'd tried the car four times, tried talking to himself too, but in a small and fearful voice that could not convince even imaginary company to stay. Ruth's presence had a wavering timidity; she was quickly gone. Frosty air edged through the single window slit open for ventilation, rose like breath from the car floor. His feet felt blue.

The sounds had started. What if a local psychopath came up here to bury something – or lived up here like a lean, mean cougar. A shadow, a ghost ... the legendary Naksup Ripper, or just the Killer. Cal could see the man: weathered face, sinewy body dressed in woollen jacket and jeans, rubber boots. Squelching through the woods each spring, drawn to civilization by his hunger. At sunset the man pauses on a ridge overlooking the valley, studies the stilling town. Sunlight glints on his silver hair, and then he turns and is not a stranger at all, but Calvin Sr, passing on down through the woods alone.

Cal snuggled into the afghan. He'd brushed against a grey-green memory, like a seaweed-entangled object. But it was the letter that was really bothering him – that was the reason for the strange image. And the fact that Calvin Sr would know what to do here, would not be so afraid. He was a man who didn't need people, who enjoyed the qualities of stone. He looked into the unseen regions of the earth and engineered the dark.

And he didn't even like Cal.

'Ach! When I was a boy, teachers were girls!'

Cast a sharp eye upon his son's belly.

Oh, Mr Van Buren, you're so strong! Women adored the old goat, even Ruth. He told them stories about the navy.

What did he want with Cal, up there in the cabin?

A wind came up. Cal listened to the forest creaking, stretching. This was a conversation, murmured in another language.

As he fell asleep, Cal plunged into another darkness, a dumb state that he knew he'd been in for a while when he woke, though it was still night. His eyes closed again. The dream started immediately. He was on a train: it was the train from Montreal to Vancouver, on which his parents had met shortly after his father came to Canada, in 1946. His mother, newly graduated from nursing school, had been going west to find work in booming British Columbia, except in the dream Cal was sitting where his mother was supposed to be: in the seat facing his father. Calvin Van Buren was young, the man from the wedding-day photographs. Dressed in his Christmas suit, he stared pensively at passing fields. He was an orphan. He carried the suitcase that had contained few possessions: a leather pipe-tobacco wallet he still used, a shaving kit, half a dozen books that Cal recalled from childhood, and a carved ivory box that Calvin later gave his fiancé as an engagement present. This was how he'd arrived, and it was all that ever came for him – no letters followed, no naval documents, no searching beam from a government office or tearful eye, no phone calls or aerograms from the country he'd left or the aunt and cousin who raised him, people who 'obviously did not survive' because they did not answer his letters and inquiries, he would later say when asked. No rumours. Never a word from anywhere, all lips and typewriters mute, as if the ship that bore him across at the end of the war had rolled up the sea behind.

As the train clattered west his father squinted at the hazy landscape, the fields of feathery wheat tips fired by the sun. Stared unwaveringly at this new country and life as if considering what these materials could fashion.

Suddenly he stood. He'd aged. He was Calvin Sr. 'Come on,' he said, motioning to Cal.

'What for?'

'This is the place.'

Cal looked out the window: there was nothing there.

'Hurry up,' his father said, picking up his suitcase.

Nervously, Cal followed his father down the aisle. The train was slowing. In one of the seats sat his mother, who grinned and waved.

He came to the end of the car and saw his father step down into a field. Cal started to follow, but stopped. The sun was red and low. He looked down at the grass and stones through the slatted iron steps under his feet. His father called impatiently. Then with anger. He was yelling at Cal, threatening punishment. But Cal knew that something worse would happen when he stepped off the train. His father needed Cal to do it. But. He wouldn't.

The whistle blew, the train rolled forward. His father's mouth went slack. His body darkened, then dwindled to a wavering black stalk in the golden field. Cal turned to find his mother but was suddenly alone, lost on the silent, undulating prairie.

When Cal opened his eyes he was dead cold. Surprisingly he could see the road through the windshield; a half-moon was glowing in the cloudy sky. Yet the ground looked strange. Cracking open the door, he pointed the flashlight: snowfall. Time check: 2:07. And the choice now between bloodthirsty wildlife and madmen, or frostbite, the latter certain.

Quietly as possible, Cal removed the plastic bags from his shoes and emerged huddled in the afghan. He retrieved his damp towel and located the path. Night enveloped him. His body sent ripples through it, the flashlight's beam disturbed. Invisible foliage brushed his legs, then something poked and he stumbled. Careful! Don't anger the trees. Cal whirled around then hurried on until his shoes resounded on wood, not even pausing to sweep the area with his flashlight before stripping off his clothes. But he couldn't enter the pool: it scalded his poor feet and hands. Overwhelmed, he curled up naked on the cold wood, splashing himself with stinging water. He longed to shrink, to become a mouse-sized man who could vanish under a leaf. At last he slipped in painfully and made for the centre of the pool, where he sank to his chin with one periscoped fist pointing the flashlight at the woods. He switched it off. The moon had gone, and he stared with mute fear into the dark as his naked body burned.

Gradually, his temperature adjusted to the pool. But once this process was over, there was nothing to indicate the passing of time. There was no time. This was eternity.

Air surged and receded. Then silence came. Both were terrible.

Cal kept thinking he saw shapes out there. He felt watched by things that normally eluded reality: wood spirits, animal people, golems that rose at night from the ground. There were footsteps, he was sure. And flickerings whenever he looked away. The flashlight showed only trees, yet the sounds and sights continued outside its light.

Once, overhead, he saw a hole with a star in it. It seemed an ancient god had retreated there and was looking down from its remote and careless remove. What if he were to die out here? Cal wondered. After his flesh had rotted or been consumed, his bones would sink to the bottom of the pool, eventually merge with it. And the world would continue turning over, pulling his bones, pulling all dead things down into the rock and mineral realm, where men (if still they existed) would delve, dusty miners scraping away their days. The mantle of life was thin, skin wrapped around rock. Everything returned to that inert underkingdom, through which the spring's water had passed.

Cal started to cry. He bit his lips to make no noise, his shoulders shaking. A puny ejaculate of tears briefly wet his cheeks. He wanted Ruth. He wanted to hear his own voice but was oppressed by the soft forest babble, by his blindness, and his fear made him ashamed. He saw his father appraising him with a cool, disgusted smirk. The man wasn't normal – why didn't he get old and sick? He had the aura of another being, an ancient one himself. He was elemental; he moulded his destiny. In an office on the Fraser River he'd drawn diagrams of service shafts and shoring, ventilation ducts, great cables and pipelines, and behold, his visions became reality. He worked and worked. Where was his gaze? Not ahead, to the future of his family; certainly not behind. Down down, toward the hidden, glittering kingdoms. He told amusing stories about the navy. He called himself Calvin Van Buren, a good Dutch name, yet he never associated with Dutch people and spoke only English, or occasionally French. Except – that day. Peculiar sharp childhood moment so strange you wish you were wrong, when Daddy was upset by a man at the door. Arguing and then shouting, so that you came out onto the landing and slid down the carpeted stairs, creeping up behind him to see. On the front step stood the man, blond and tall like Daddy. They spoke a foreign language; you thought it must be Dutch. And then the man noticed you and said hello in a friendly way. He said, 'I'm your uncle,' and smiled.

Daddy wheeled. Wild, frightened eyes.

You feared for your life.

'Pieter, you should not be this way,' the man said in English.

What is Pieter? you wondered. Was it like Doctor? A name for someone special?

The man was sent away. In a little while Daddy came looking. Such nonsense, he said. The man owed him money and wanted more, that was why he wasn't invited in for coffee or a glass of wine like other guests. The man was no good! Foolish, always making things up, the kind of fellow who expects others to solve his problems. They should set an animal trap in the yard to keep him out! Daddy became jolly and laughed about the incident. He looked at you, and you felt you were supposed to laugh too, and did. It was a relief to, even if you knew it was a lie.

The truth was, Father was inside a box. For a moment, the lid had been ripped open.

What was inside the box with him? What had he taken there to protect with those terrible, violent eyes?

Cal's own eyes were wide in the dark. His father, he knew, was not a living man. He was a dead one with a new name. That's what they did, the guilty; they erased themselves. His father was a black hole, and now at last he was calling out: needing love and understanding, needing forgiveness, needing a witness. A sacrifice. Life. Cal's life.

In the woods, in the dark, his father had brought him to this place of preparation. But Cal would deny him. He would hide forever.

With a whimper Cal gulped a last breath and sank until he touched the bottom of the pool, where still he sensed his father's hands passing and repassing over the waters above, searching, searching, until at last, weakened, they withdrew, leaving Cal alone in solitary warmth. Safe.

* * *

Cal was lucky. He didn't die. He lived like a frog, surfacing and sinking again and again in the water, and eventually he saw night's phantoms routed by the plain, comprehensible day. The trees stood dumbly. His watch gave the time. In the flat light of a grey dawn he descended the mountainside, a cold and tired wreck of a man again but with a faint confidence that, when he sighted the highway and knew he would soon be in town, surged to survival pride. And as he stepped down from the delivery truck that drove him right to the lodge, bearing him like a returning champion to Ruth, that pride grew and began to enfold the night's stark experience.

The enfolding continued as the years passed, the story of his night trapped on the mountain becoming a family legend he retold with delight. The letter from his father received a polite and brief reply, the invitation to the cabin declined because Cal was a busy man and his vacations were all planned; but they would see each other at Christmas, and on Mother's birthday. Ruth was unusually vocal about Cal's behaviour here, going so far as to say she was appalled that he could so cruelly slight a lonely old man. But Cal didn't budge, and Calvin Sr became a topic they avoided. Cal took up bird watching. He learned about nature with a group of ambling naturalists, one of whom was a lively divorced lady who liked Cal very much, and although in twenty-three years of marriage Cal had never had an affair, once he began he

felt more vital than ever, his life charged with energy. One afternoon
he was hiking with his group, and his lover, and decided that even
when the affair ended there could be another woman. It was all right.
Cal stopped and looked up the trunk of a magnificent red alder. That's
me, he thought: tapped into a strength that's lain dormant too long.
He was growing surely, growing into the man he always knew he
could be.

This Side of Thirty

I fall in love with Marty Stein at La Bodega Tapas Restaurant, though I can't admit this to myself until later, at home.

On the sofa, hugging my knees, I stare at the carpet and sip the Cabernet left over from my roommate Vera's date. A simmering candle gives our living room a churchly glow that also reminds me of La Bodega's stucco grotto, where Marty and I sat tonight. Marty, the Stein boy. Of all people.

I suppose it began a few months ago when Marty moved to Vancouver and we started getting together to yak and exchange complaints, usually over pitchers of sangria at La Bodega. Our families: how they're so *them*, and we're so *us*. Though our connection was old and overgrown with adult distance, it ran deep, and those first few visits I found myself welcoming Marty as a kind of comrade-in-arms, a co-conspirator. There was delight and an unexpected mystery and in rediscovering my childhood friend far from Montreal. Falling into slouchy, retrograde habits during family visits with Steins, I'd more or less ignored Marty for the last fifteen years. And given his ludicrous teenage romance with my sister Dahlia, an expert at dramatized mundanity, in this case their utterly predictable breakup when they moved away to separate universities, followed by her marriage and Marty's drift into a peripatetic career of tree-planting and working for one-computer non-profits, I think dismissal was excusable. Yet somewhere between last Christmas and the Vancouver airport, Marty changed. There was the position with the Suzuki Foundation, even a better haircut, and more: he'd stopped apologizing. I sensed a man with new dimensions; hidden roots, depths.

'Well, Mart,' I announced tonight, the liquor and soft cha-cha tunes making me bold, 'I'm sure glad you've come. I'm glad I'm not to be alone out here any more.' My hand floated toward his thigh and touched warm denim. Marty flashed me one of his shy-boy grin (how could I have withstood that?) and looked into his glass. Some long –

chasteningly long – seconds passed, and I took my hand away. We left soon after, the blocks to the bus stop slow torture, but all embarrassment and doubt removed by Marty's tight, lingering hug goodbye.

Of course it's mutual.

I finish the wine. Pinch the wick and step toward the living room window, remembering the firmness of Marty's thigh as I peer out at the city lights. Desire, I must also remember, is a trickster. Yet this feels different, more *sensible,* which is not a word I've normally found attractive when linked with romance, a word more likely to come from my mother's mouth, spoken with confidence and, I suppose, possibly wisdom. The Steins and my parents are best friends; the Stein kids practically grew up with us. His thing with Dahlia is ancient history, and my only feeling about it now is amusement. So when it comes down to it, the rightness of the match is unarguable. Marty could be my perfect mate.

Mate. Now there's a word with weight, finality. A word to feel in your chest. Using the windowsill to balance I raise myself on my toes, feel poised on the verge of a great drop or leap.

As I wobble down the hall to bed, I indulge in a voyeuristic pause at Vera's door. Our all-female, half-serious rock band, the White Panties, has been dried up for a while, yet occasional gigs at dyke bars and charity events still reel in the babes. The foreign pair of women's shoes on the landing have already told me Vera's scored, she's in there with tonight's date, a woman who looks just like her.

Isn't there always a sibling edge to love?

In my belly these days is the hollow ache I've named the Void. I feel it most consistently in the morning, when I open my eyes to the walls of my room and think: still this? It's not like boredom, or restlessness. Strange, how emptiness can throw you off balance. The Void appeared six months ago when I was back in Montreal, perched on the sofa arm during our family's Christmas Day thing. Dad stepped back from the tripod and waved us all closer. Forced cheer amid smells of roasting meat and potatoes. I remember my irritation at being squeezed between Dahlia and a tittering sister-in-law, and a fleeting puzzlement at how maturity had brought us a new kind of childish awkwardness. The men, wearing their woollen holiday sweaters and forming a wall behind us, either laughed or coughed. Perfume disagreed with cologne. No one likes these pictures, yet every year the same routine: snapshot chronicle of our mortality, our little greying clan. Dad waved a hand at me before rushing to his spot: 'Look here, Lizzy. Lizzy!'

An eye, a burst of light. Smarting seconds, then back to normal with the general assembly at table. I stayed where I was. What had just happened? Light had flashed and gone out; that was all. Yet something had changed. *The bottom's fallen out,* I'd thought, wondering what this meant.

After supper the Steins came over as they always do, relieving us with their conviviality, yet I slunk away early. Two days later I flew back to Vancouver confused, even teary at times. Across the aisle a baby mewled, its mother adjusted her sweater to feed. I felt weak at the glimpse of breast, the nipple raw as the child's mouth opening to clasp it. My blood thrummed with a primitive desire, stronger than hunger or lust: me too. What had suddenly seemed so urgent and necessary as I'd sat on that sofa was children. Family. Life. Life! I was fervid with the desire for it, and no one could tell. But really, I countered, *moi?* The prospect was bizarre, even risible – yet enthralling. Feathery clouds passed my window like cherubs' wings. I rattled peanuts and magazines but kept smelling milk, infant hair, folded infant skin.

At work, I basically don't give a shit any more. Eventually this is what always happens: I calculate the end-date of my patience, save like hell, and maintain sanity by planning a gloriously long trip with my guitar to some far-flung corner of the globe. When that's over I slink back and find work again.

I'm thirty-four.

From across the open-concept office, Jed, our photo researcher, regards me soulfully. I've considered dating him, but ever since Christmas, entanglements with men, be they casual, serial, or prolonged dances of 'friendship' – in other words, my littered past – have seemed silly. I'm loath to admit it, but romance, as I've enacted it, seems adolescent.

Appearing brisk and busy under Jed's gaze, I surf my favourite web sites: Lonely Planet, Mojo Magazine, the Vatican Museum, Discovery on-line; sites on weather, on metalworking, seventies fashion styles, North American archaeology and coastal birds ... I have a brain like a curiosity shop.

Marty answers after I call him twice in a row; that's our code. He shares my distaste for phones and a surprising number of other affinities, such as my enthusiasm for what Dahlia, with a nasty laugh, once termed 'the realms of the safely obscure'.

I tell Marty what I've found today: a site on Canada's buried treasure mystery, Oak Island, Nova Scotia.

'Oh yeah, I've read about that,' he says, and then he tells me about a boat trip he took out East once all by himself to look at shoreline caves. I smile as he talks; his voice is still throaty, sleep-tender.

'Do you want to meet me for lunch?' I blurt, just like that. Considering my hand-on-thigh went nowhere the other night, I wouldn't normally be this assertive, not with another man. But Marty isn't another man: he's Mart, and we used to play Aliens vs. Earthlings and dress up as KISS in his parents' rec room.

'What time is it?'

'Ten. We'll call it brunch for you.'

Jed passes close to my cubicle. I curl the phone cord around my finger and lower my voice, intoning with as much sex appeal as I dare. 'So, are you going to come?'

'Tell me where,' Marty says.

It's challenging to feel excited about life when sex and men stop being adventures, when you don't know what the hell it is you're trying to do any more and you're haunted not by visions of music-making in Costa Rica, but the solid weight of a baby slung against your chest. Its softness and warmth, its gooey mouth, the demented jabs of its sharp little nails. And then, the impossibility of exchanging my lifestyle for the nuclear family cloister, with its asphyxiation of joy by daycares, debts, driving, and silent resentment. Yes, I'm a spoiled thing.

One evening a few weeks ago, when I was in an especially black mood and had not yet fallen in love, when I thought I was merely enjoying the much-needed fellowship of a family-like person with whom I could actually connect, I called Marty and asked him to meet me at La Bodega. He wore jeans faded to patchy whiteness and a prickly cable-knit sweater that looked left over from his tree-planting years. When he folded himself into the chair, his torso towered over the table and his head knocked one of the stucco outcrop 'rocks' on the grotto walls. He let out a wonderfully goofy laugh.

This boy-man surrendered his virginity to Dahlia, I thought. He shared a sacred moment with a woman who looked at all life had to offer and chose to use her intelligence and talent to facilitate corporate investment banking.

Sometime when we were on our second pitcher, the conversation swung around to our families again. I told Marty about that Christmas Day photo, which my mother later sent. Despite all the squeezing our family fit easily into the frame: dwindling humanoid cluster, clinging to that couch like a rock.

I said, 'Don't you think it's bizarre that none of my siblings has children?' I counted off on my fingers. 'Married, monied, suburban, addicted to cars and TV. All the bulwarks of middleclassdom, yet no offspring. Isn't that weird? They can't all be infertile.'

Marty sucked a wine-soaked slice of orange, peeled off the rind. 'Families exist to be inexplicable,' he observed. I liked this new, epigrammatic side to him.

'Have you talked to them about it?'

'Sure. Of course, they won't give any meaningful answers. Whenever I ask my brothers about it, they say they're 'too busy' and tell me to have a kid myself if I'm so keen.'

'And Dahlia?' he said more carefully.

'She says she has two cats and a husband and that's enough. I mean, why get married? Why own two vehicles and a three-bedroom house?' I eyed the red depths of my glass, feeling a sudden anxiety. 'Do you think there could be something fateful about it? What if certain tendencies run in families? Depression, infidelity ... in this case, a kind of self-extinction gene. A will to die out?' This thought had just struck me and seemed to explain much, though it would be terrible news.

Marty cocked his head. 'We speak of family trees, and every real tree eventually dies. Either it gets toppled by an external event, a storm or saw, or –'

'Something internal happens.'

We sat quietly for a while. I was sliding back into the bleary mood I'd come out to escape. Monday night and Jobim crooning 'The Girl from Ipanema' to empty tables. Then I remembered that a year ago I'd been in this same room, possibly at the same table, on my penultimate date with Jacob, my old boyfriend. What on earth had possessed me to bring Marty here? The clichéd music and campy fixtures oozed futility.

Marty started to laugh.

'Do you remember the summer you stayed at our cottage and we built that huge fort outside?'

'Fort?' I blinked, misty-eyed.

Marty described the cardboard boxes with rough, cut-out windows, our rag curtains. As we pilfered from his parents' shed, our fort grew into an entire colony interconnected with ground-level 'escape hatches' between boxes.

I frowned. 'Didn't we have a box of stolen Kotex?'

'You used them to make "war bandages". You were hilarious! You marched next door to our neighbour wearing one on your forehead and asked him for a cardboard box.'

'Did I?' I said, impressed with this child. Images of those days were surfacing: Marty and me squatting over a pond, watching tadpoles flick like shadows. And then a quieter scene on the fort's grassy floor, while somewhere outside the distant drone of a mower, the sound of summer. Huddled face to face, our noses and then our lips touching. Playing parents.

Helplessly delighted, I smiled and put my hands to my cheeks, still feeling that shelter.

At Fix Media's so-trendy Yaletown office I actually do some work to pass the time before lunch. The owners of Fix seem to think a person really needs thirty-five hours a week to condense blathery government and industry reports into these little newsletters and booklets, which the designers make resemble lifestyle magazines. Effective pacing and subtle self-promotion help me maintain an illusion of productivity and devote a chunk of company time to clicking through photos of the Galapagos Islands, the *Utne Reader* on-line.

A gabby circle of employees hovers near the coffee counter with work in their hands. My co-workers spend hours flirting with bike couriers or discussing hair dye. Only a few are married with families. Everyone else is relishing the money, the freedom.

Jed, also an artistic photographer and really quite an attractive guy, comes over to my corner. As we're conferring about some cuts to one of my blurbs there's another, mute conversation going on, where he says, 'I'm going to stand this close to you. What are you going to do about it?' And he does, his skin smelling of bergamot and romance. And I say, 'Whatever.' Then, flipping through a ministry report no one will ever read, he says, 'I'm going to lean a little so my shoulder – note its firmness – unnecessarily grazes yours. What are you going to do about it?' I do nothing. Am I nuts?

Some figures to consider:

A. In perhaps six years, my ovaries, like store-bought cartons of eggs, will officially expire. They'll be 'off'.

B. Six months ago, my roommate Vera was in love with a man.

C. My hairdresser's recent suggestion: Highlights would cover your ten per cent grey.

D. One year ago I was in love, or so I thought, with Jacob.

Who still occasionally leaves cryptic messages in my voice mail. Jacob wanted us to live together, have a kid or two, and I'd hear none of it. Why the fuck would I do that? The White Panties had half a CD's worth of songs we'd recorded (still only half). I wanted to move to Europe, teach French in Yellowknife, cycle across Iceland, write my memoirs in a kibbutz tent.

Two years here, six months there, new boyfriends and distractions, same old. We all have our addictions, and apparently, mine is choice.

Striding down Denman Street to the Japanese Noodle Café, I try to convince myself that I've got to be the most mouth-watering woman Marty's ever known. Besides looking hot, who else would enthusiastically gab about Oak Island – or pirate lore, string theory, dystopian films, Vikings, *The Prisoner*, Captain Beefheart, famous shipwrecks of the Great Lakes? 'Realms of the safely obscure'? Our leaping conversations are the stuff of life! Jungle romps through the wonders of the world.

In the crowded café I locate Marty's looming torso immediately. A few men look vulnerable when they see me. My hair's loose and I've dressed up today: slim black skirt, red blouse. Power colours.

Marty rises and kisses my cheek, something he's not done before. His hand holds mine for a moment, and when we're seated there's a lovely flush over his face. This is a date, I think. It's a time we'll be looking back on soon, talking about how awkward we both were. But then Marty sighs, rubs his forehead, and when a waitress places a bowl of cloudy miso before him, he tosses back his tea like a shot and asks for more.

'Working late last night?'

'No, not really.' His eyes slide distractedly around the room, his leg joggles. I'm uneasy: usually Marty has the hopeful, fizzy energy of a kid messing with a chemistry set. At last he says, 'It's just that I've been wondering about this place, Vancouver. I don't want to prejudge, but I'm not sure I can live here. It's really not what I expected.'

'It's not Montreal?'

'No, of course not.'

Now we both look around the room. Though every table's occupied, there's a hushed atmosphere that seems to emanate from the undersized furniture and discreet halogen lighting, the clinical efficiency of the slender, oval-faced waitresses.

Marty fingers his lower lip. Then straightens, arms across chest, and looks me in the eye. I feel a bit faint. How could I have wasted years dating hip, cool men, when it's this combination of geekiness and control, the man and the child, that seduces?

He says, 'I guess I expected, well, more passion.'

I raise my eyebrows.

He takes a gulp of miso, exhales and momentarily shuts his eyes. 'You know, that *je ne sais quoi,* that West Coast spirit or whatever it is you hear about. Where is it?' He leans forward, cranking up. 'This place – the land – is awesomely beautiful. When I look out my window in the morning and see clouds floating over the rocky peaks, changing the light every second, and then the water stretching to the horizon, and the ground so lush and alive, I know I'm being summoned to open my eyes, to learn something important. But what do I do? I walk around the city and lose that feeling, because the city's completely out of synch. Downtown's tiny and new. Chain stores dominate. The architecture's mostly ugly. There's barely any feeling of history or culture, except maybe in Chinatown. The only time I feel excited again is when I walk across the Burrard Street Bridge, or around the Stanley Park seawall. The West End's probably fun if you're gay, but otherwise, I don't get this place. Maybe I'm missing something.'

'You're missing an essential point, Mart. People don't move here for the city, they move here to be *out* of the city. This is a city of back-packers, kayakers, biologists, hippies, hikers, bikers, skiers and wanna-be Gulf Island survivalists – you follow? There's no energy left for culture because it's all directed elsewhere. This grid's just a waysta-tion, where you make money and spend it.'

As I'm speaking a terrific idea comes to me. 'You know what the problem is?' I lean closer, resisting the urge to take Marty's hand. 'You need an infusion of the "outside" part. Get away. Fall in love –' I meet his eyes and see a little jolt there '– with the mountains.' Before he can respond I spring my plan: camping, this weekend, at Garibaldi Park. I promise to arrange everything.

Marty grins. Yet he doesn't answer right away. I let him mull it over, and when I get home that night his message is waiting.

'Where you going?'

Lounging at the kitchen table in loose, bosomy bath robes, Vera and her new lover grin at me like twins. With their dark eyes and furry, tightly cropped heads, they resemble some cute variety of herbivore.

'Garibaldi.' I grunt, extracting gear from our suite's one storage closet.

'That's great!' Lover says, this woman who walks around in trekking boots and brings pepper plants for our windowsill. 'Who you going with?' she asks eagerly. Just being friendly, I guess.

'With Marty.' I tug at the nylon sleeve containing my tent. Stacked milk crates full of albums shudder. Bands from high school and university days, toted by Vera and me east to west and from rental to rental like hearth stones.

'Oh. The Stein boy,' Vera says, with a note of disappointment. My inaction on the dating front's been puzzling her.

'Who's the Stein boy?'

'Lightbulb Head. Friend of the family.'

'I don't call him that any more,' I say, ashamed. 'He's actually changed a lot. He's pretty amazing.'

Vera stares at me. 'You aren't thinking of him as romance material, are you?' She gulps her coffee. Her cheeks bulge and blow air. 'Jesus. Liz.'

'What? I really like him. You've got a tainted view.'

She turns to Lover. 'He deflowered her sister.'

'Oh my God.'

Vera shakes her head. 'What is it with this guy?'

Within an hour I'm behind a rental car wheel, idling outside of Marty's apartment on Marine Drive. Across the road at Spanish Banks, the shapes of joggers and dog walkers interrupt the morning haze. Soon enough, couples will arrive for picnics and beach games with their children. I'm continually amazed that otherwise conservative people gamble so much – home and identity and kids (those trusting ignorant beings, those other dependent lives) – on romance. How can something so irrational, so sandcastle whimsical and above all impractical be the basis of house and home, what is hilariously called 'security'? But my love for Marty? No, that's not the same; we're not two unknowns betting on what's really behind each other's curtains. That's why the perfection of my plan thrills me. I see us coming here in a few years, two kindred souls forever united by history and temperament and a child. Ours will be a truly creative union, a mutual exploration of existence rather than a joint acquisition project. And we'll still have our adventures, of course, treks to Nepal and teaching stints in Prague, only together. And we'll –

I stop. A thought like a cold breeze blowing from the future whispers, *No way*. It won't happen. You won't get off that easily.

I grip the wheel. Get off from what?

Marty swings out the door, backpack bouncing as he strides down the drive. He nears the car. Yet until the door clunks open I'm certain he won't stop. No, he'll continue walking right though me. I can't stop him. I can't move. I'm old now, still living with Vera in our tiny two-bedroom (two childless crones). And all this was just a time, a once. A time of temporary hope, or madness.

The coastal road swerves around the mountainsides, showing us valleys and hazy green islands and once in a while waves of mountains extending north. Between gulps of scenery Marty amuses me by reading aloud from a library book on the history of the Squamish mine. No date of mine would ever dream of doing such a weird thing; boyfriends have flattered and flat-out adored, but none ever tried to woo my brain.

I head for the Chekamus Lake trail, a woodland meander to a snug, waterside clearing with a few camp sites. But at the turnoff a sign says the trail's closed. No problem, I tell Mart, Garibaldi's full of trails. We drive on to Whistler and pick up a park guide. Shoulders together, we eat the sandwiches I packed and study our options.

'How about this one?'

'Wedgemount. I don't know it. It says "extreme difficulty".'

'Oh. Right.' Marty gives me a concerned look.

'But hey, that's fine with me,' I say. 'Those warnings are bogus, anyway. They're just trying to scare away seniors and families.' I grin cavalierly and start the car. Trying a new trail with Marty seems right, after all. We reach the trail head in a few minutes, and I'm surprised to see a dozen SUVs and jeeps. I hoist my pack, stagger, and follow Marty's lead.

Wedgemount trail begins as a relentless climb, a zigzagging trudge up a slope like a hundred flights of uneven stairs. But I'm in great shape, I tell myself, watching my footwork on the rooty soil. My thighs burn. Buggy black specks orbit my head. Above us the green canopy rustles, but on the path we're enclosed in a cedar-chest stillness. Marty hikes too fast.

After almost an hour I call a halt and collapse on a log to devour fistfuls of trail mix. Marty paces, hands on hips. He exudes the canine energy of fit men in the midst of a workout. Suddenly he comes over and lays a hand on my shoulder, then starts to massage my neck. I shut my eyes. I picture his fingers rubbing my hair and skin.

'You all right? You're looking a bit green.'

'I'm fine,' I reply, not knowing what I'm saying. His hand seems to be all around me, I'm curling up in its hollow.

Marty gives me a final squeeze and resumes pacing. On we go then. I stand up, refreshed and eager to reach the top.

The trail keeps ascending in leg-stretching lifts, and then we reach a greystone scree and veer south on level ground. Fanned by a slight breeze now we pass through a wood filled with enormous ferns, nature-sized versions of those frilly bursts of green hung as humanizing afterthoughts in offices. We emerge onto a scruffy, near-vertical slope. The sunlit summit sways a little against the sky. The path goes up.

'Oh God,' I moan.

'Unbelievable,' Marty says.

A thin, snaky trail now, dry and stony. The slope forces us to bend over and steady the climb with our hands. I heave and pant and sweat and swat at bugs and dwell on the sanctuary of the tent to come. Finally the summit nears, and after a last scramble, we're up. Up! For a moment all we can do is stare at the scene, it's so unusual. The word I think of first is *remote*. Before us lies a flat, almost bare, football-field-sized plateau; not the summit at all, but the end of the trail. What little vegetation grows here is dwarfed, humbled. Rising on three sides are the icy flanks of mountains whose peaks are quite near. Glaciers reach right to the plateau's perimeter. There is a hushed silence and privacy about this place. The afternoon sun has already left it in shadow.

I've forgotten about the cars in the parking lot, but now I realize that we're not alone. Near the trail head is a cheery cluster of tents, like a frontier camp. Bodies sway up the glaciers using poles. Pot in hand, a woman swishes past us in all-weather pants and skids down a gravel slope to a pale, slushy pool at the bottom.

'My God,' Marty whispers.

I shiver, and take his hand.

Marty's fingers press mine, but then he moves away, turning a full circle. 'This is amazing! You were so right, Liz. I can't believe it.'

'You're happy, then?'

In response he laughs and turns around more. 'It's like photographs I've seen of Tibet. And how far away from the city? A few hours? People pay thousands to get to places like this! I've gone to South America and Asia to see this.' His eyes shine.

I smile, and leave him to enjoy himself while I start setting up the tent. I can't stake it on the rocks, so have to hunt for stones. You'd think this would be easy but there seem to be none, the gravel too small, and everything else too large or nabbed by the other campers. I end up returning to the summit path. On the hillface I teeter with my load and catch some rays from the setting sun. Far westward a shimmering line slits the sky: the Georgia Strait.

For dinner I assemble crackers with brie, then a mushroom risotto with steamed vegetables. Dressed in fleece sweaters, Marty and I sit on our sleeping bags outside, while from Tent Town, bits of conversation and laughter reach us between mouthfuls, floating on the silence like wafts of heat in frosty air. Marty offers random observations about glaciation, prehistoric North Americans, the Clovis/pre-Clovis debates, yet my responses feel sobered by this place and the question mark of the night to come.

'So Mart, do you think we'll freeze tonight?' I say.

He shrugs. 'Don't know. Maybe they'll find us in ten thousand years.' He slaps his knees, rises and – shit, he's not coming closer, he's heading away, toward the wooden outhouse that stands dolmen-like near the slope of that eerie, ice-blue pool.

While he's gone, I'm visited by the ghosts of former boyfriends. *Have* I fucked up? Missed the right opportunity, been spoiled by choice, by pleasures? My life seems as lean as string, with random tangles, patches of activity and passion and attempts at creation that have all petered to thinness.

I go off with my toothbrush and water, and when I return to our tent I find the lantern on, Marty zipped up tight in his bag and reading. I close the flap and start unlacing my boots. Marty looks up.

'Hey,' he says.

'Hey yourself.' I put aside my boots and toothbrush and lie down, staring at the tent's ceiling. The various ploys I can conjure to get closer to Marty strike me as false. I've moved away from that past; now is the time to be an adult, to put aside games and speak from the heart.

Marty asks if I'm sleepy. No, I say. I squeeze shut my eyes, open them again.

'Marty. There's no casual way to say this. I think I've fallen in love with you.'

Into the chasm of the next moment I hold out hope, first with confidence, and then, as the moment extends and Marty neither moves nor speaks, but simply gawks, with apparent agitation on his face, I begin to hear my words coming back to me and they do not sound either adult or well chosen, but passionless and blunt. Perhaps I should have explained. Perhaps I should have just semi-modestly undressed, allowing him to observe the removal of bra from under the shirt, for example, before finding a pretext to snuggle up next to him.

And perhaps Marty doesn't want honesty at all.

I sit up. 'Okay, that was obviously –'

Marty reaches out a hand but doesn't touch me. 'No, Liz, I'm sorry. I'm just shocked.' He sits up too.

'Shocked? You're *shocked*? Marty, we're two single people who seem to have this great connection, and we've been hanging out for months.'

'I know. You're right. I don't mean shock. It's that I don't know what to do about it. I never, ever expected this. When I came here, I mean.'

'Well neither did I.'

We're both quiet for a moment. Marty's wearing a snug thermal shirt that reveals the lineaments of his arms and shoulders, and it seems to me that his body, if only it could be set in motion, would release such pleasures, would create a new and vital world for us to live in. I move to crouch before him and have barely touched one side of his face when his hands push mine away. He turns and runs his hands through his hair. I retreat and make myself small, arms around knees.

Then I have to listen to Marty telling me how he's terribly sorry. How I'm lovely, I'm wonderful. And that he's fond of me, sexually attracted to me too, yes, that's true. But he doesn't want to 'get involved'.

'Liz, you've been an unexpected comfort since I got here, an amazing friend.' He looks at me sharply. 'And I know I probably gave you mixed messages. It's hard not too. But, that's just men and women, you know?'

'Oh. Them.'

'I have to be really honest here: I have contemplated this. And I just don't see you that way in my life. I never have. I mean, you're Dahlia's sister, and all that was ages ago. You're … part of the family. You're like a cousin.'

'Uh-huh.' Who would have thought that would be a strike against? I look around the watery tent. Dignity's abandoning me. Where's the escape hatch?

'I think that we – Liz? Liz!'

I'm already half gone. Lurch through the flap into the night and start walking, boots in hand. When I'm sure Marty's not following I stop to slip them on. I don't bother with the laces. I'm living dangerously now.

Under a blaze of stars, I shuffle across the lunar plateau toward the black peaks with their ghostly swathes of ice. Tears slide sharp and cold down my cheeks. The air slips inside my shirt and starts alarming my skin, making the hairs bristle. Up here the ice age is still in full swing, whether anyone cares or knows.

Not far to the end of the plateau. What now? I stomp onto the edge of a glacier, kick sparks of ice. Then I walk back to the rocky ground and lean against a boulder, sniffling. Across the plateau Tent Town is a huddle of phosphorescent humps, and I can see our own tent separated from the rest and faintly glowing. I imagine myself continuing to sit here immobile though the night, until my blood hardens and my eyelashes go white and I become a beautiful statue of myself, a final and solitary creation.

After a while I become aware of an increase in light: the moon is rising from behind the mountains. I wait for it, watching my breath stream, and when she brilliantly appears I'm startled by her great size, her nearness and stark nudity. And then, something odd happens on the ground near my feet. What's this? A skittering like pebbles; pause, and again. I squat down, and see them: white mice are darting about, foraging for things to nibble in the soil. Wanting to offer something, I hold out a bare hand until a mouse approaches and noses the end of one finger. It's a ticklish touch, a secret and thrilling pleasure. In the moonlight the mouse's eyes glitter like polished stones.

Nine Outtakes from the Life of Mark T.

1.

Whenever he tells the story it changes. During the first account, he knows where he's editing. At a party some people are discussing a recent child abduction case, and Mark contributes his story as another example of social menace. He emphasizes the brevity of the phone call – an instant of inattention – and his panic. Did his girlfriend freak? Freak doesn't come close, but what mother wouldn't? He totally understands, knows why she couldn't forgive him.

There's sympathy, mostly. One woman, a small, unnoteworthy blonde, sends him a look of pure disdain, and the rest of the evening he pursues her. She's turns out to be actually quite interesting. For the next few days, he even thinks he might like to see her again.

2.

Mark is hunched at his desk, studying three credit cards lined under a metal lamp. November 12, 2004: it's a day of unexpected joy, for they arrived in the morning post and Dep has just delivered them.

Oh my children, Mark thinks. You wafers of gold.

He leans back in his chair for another perspective on the names he created, now ridged in plastic: John T. Woo, Martin Brando, Serge Leone. Mark's brood – though as a nod to his superior imagination, Dep let Mark choose the names for all eight offspring, the octet of identities sprung from their combined skills over months of tricky manoeuvring. Five for Dep, who obtained the IDs and plotted the banking strategies, and three for apprenticing Mark, who managed the accounts.

He's both inside and outside, understands the middle and the edges. Long ago he realized that life, to be truly known, must be learned independently and rigorously, through testing and risk. Feel violence is wrong? Crime doesn't pay? Try, then see.

Most people are numbed by the sanitized, pre-packaged life they unconsciously choose, suffering a kind of white blindness whose anti-dote is darkness. That's why they rush to films full of brutality, raunchy sex, crime, death. The churches are empty, the cinemas full. But even with less ignorance, they'd still rush to the screens. Why? Because people's deepest desire, Mark believes, is to see themselves mirrored. Everyone yearns to be the statue in the town square, the face chiselled into the mountain. Thus, film is possibly the greatest technological invention, though its potential has been only partially realized. Who could have imagined that people would be able to see themselves as *animated* statues? With film, it's as if a person becomes their own avatar.

He'd put that line in the script once. Two guys meet in a small town coffee shop: one is a young, oh-so-cool filmmaker scouting locations for his next project, the other a middle-aged preacher who's seen everything. The preacher gets the line.

Everything goes into his writing. A crystallization of purpose occurred when he read a statement by a Swedish poet who said that three things are necessary for the artist to flourish: (i) awareness, (ii) a life arranged to allow sufficient time for dedication to one's craft, and (iii) technique. Schools teach only the last of these. University courses, those he attended, merely confirmed their own irrelevance. What made Shakespeare great? Language united with the fullest spectrum of human reality: the highs and lows, insanity and nobility, kings and commoners.

After almost a decade of dedication to his craft, the work's about to pay off. Mark can feel the energy gathered about him like a charge: he will sell a script this year.

Like a croupier Mark sweeps up the cards and clacks them against the desk, presents them splayed to an imaginary player, them re-deals. Hunkers down with his chin on his knuckles.

'Welcome to the world, kids,' he whispers, lips puckering into a grin. If he can pawn the equipment he's going to buy for decent prices, manage the monthly payments until the cards are maxed and still sell some dope, these boys will be his ticket to six months of focused writing time – his own arts grant.

He reaches out and strokes each card with his index finger. Plastic glossy as oil. Making life just slide open.

3.

He was supposed to take care of Chad. Instead, he lost him.

He's shown them where. Described everything. A search of the beach and surrounding area is being organized, but the officer who interviewed him, name-tagged Wilson, keeps asking questions, though Mark is goose-pimpled and shivering in his corduroy shirt and jeans. There's no protection out here.

'Where's your coat?'

'I didn't bring one.'

More judgmental silence.

The man's not only unsympathetic and mean, he's suspicious, Mark thinks. Why scrutinize my ID? He ran it through the system, and what if something came back? A file, a *dossier*.

What do I really know about Allan?

Or Dep?

It would be Dep: a guy with too much going on, credit card fraud being just one revenue stream in a whole pirating industry. And what if there are other dealings that Dep's not mentioned? Like on-line porn?

Oh God. *Kiddie* porn.

Mist swirling in the cruiser's headlights, coating the men's skin. Officer Wilson continuing to write in a wire-bound book. There are cops all around them now, their cars blocking the narrow road. Men are gathering to walk the length of the point in formation. Powerful flashlights sweep the sand.

Mark gazes at the ocean, a blackness unbroken until low on the horizon where a faint grey light glows, reminding him for a moment that children, like anyone, may be seized by forces more potent than human evil, human error. But you can't tell that to the cops. What can he? The 911 call was straightforward enough. He admires the response time. But what was he doing way out here this time of day, Wilson wants to know. Mark had prepared an answer to that:

plane watching. I took the boy to see the planes.

Coatless. In December.

'Okay,' Wilson says, stopping his pen. 'Why did you wait so long before calling us?'

'Was it? I didn't realize it was so long. I was losing it out here.' Nice wording, stupid, he thinks, almost shaking his head.

The officer flips back in his notebook and reads. 'You said the disappearance happened at approximately 4:15 p.m. Your call came in at 7:17 p.m.' He looks at Mark. 'Almost three hours.'

Mark remembers: wandering up and down the shore, shouts that died on the wind. The sky darkening.

'Something like this happens,' the officer is saying, 'it's damn serious. Right?' He glares until Mark feels compelled to nod.

'So you call the police IMMEDIATELY. You DON'T try to sort it out yourself. You DON'T try to play the hero.'

'I just thought –'

'If you'd called us right away, we might have located the suspect on the highway. We might have your girlfriend's boy back already. You see?'

'Yes.' Mark shuts his eyes for a moment.

'Good. I hope that's clear. Now, why didn't you phone ... Ms Cho, right away?'

Eunice. He can't picture her clearly now, though often images of her obsess him. He can still sense his feelings for her, but ever since the police arrived (no, since he made the 911 call, that surrendering of effort), the connection's gone slack.

'I didn't want to scare her,' he says. 'I thought Chad was hiding.'

'That's not what you said?'

'I thought he might be. I don't know kids,' Mark says, anxiety giving way to exasperation. 'Look, what good would it do to freak her out? I realize I wasn't thinking very clearly. I just thought I'd be able to find him.'

'Well, I suggest you call her now. Either the news comes from you or from me.' Mark looks down at his cell phone, which he's been gripping. For another moment Wilson continues to watch him, then lets it go. 'You got half the suspect's licence plate and a clear physical description. That's a good start. Hopefully, that'll help us.' He thanks Mark and moves off, negotiating the sand with purposeful steps, his body equipped with instruments and weapons. A father, Mark thinks, and with a slow slackening of tension realizes that what he thought was suspicion was judgment of a deeper sort.

The search team has now travelled far up the beach, their beams of light meeting and separating in the dark as regularly as the waves on the sand.

4.

He's got a million things on his plate. The script's at a crucial stage. He needs to buy another laptop to sell so he can inject some cash into his account to make his rent and phone and minimum credit card payments, and to have in pocket for all the little transactions that still require it: public transit, the basement bike repair shop, drugs, personal debts and the like. There's coffee next week with a director wanting to discuss a script Mark's been marketing for years and should glance at again, while another's about to be optioned. His hotmail account's clogged. A party where he might meet a filmmaker looking for a story similar to what he's working on is happening tonight, which means tracking down an acquaintance to get an invite. There are the week's notes, fragments of overheard dialogue, reflections and odd sightings, hastily scribbled and soon to be indecipherable if he doesn't write them out. Eunice has been bugging him to go out for dinner. He forgot Mother's Day, once again.

Yet at 2:45, when he's supposed to be writing or at the very least accomplishing something on the list, Mark's speeding up Marine Drive in his roommate's ancient Honda Civic to meet Allan Petrynko at Iona Beach for three o'clock. The car keeps cutting out; some wayward valve, apparently. Buckled in the back seat atop a stack of phone books so he can see out the window is Chad, the blunt black dome of his head rotating in curious scans of his environment.

Mark glances at him in the rearview.

The boy is three, though to Mark Chad might as well be any age between one and twelve. Teenagers interest him; that's where real life seems to start, lurching into the stark ambitions that just grow subtler over time. But children – a vague category of life.

What *is* Chad, Mark has occasionally wondered. The boy doesn't say much. He likes cereal. Can he tie his own laces? Wipe his bum? Mark's not sure. There's so little to this person. He's a smudge on a page, waiting to become an outline.

It doesn't help that Mark's barely seen Chad during the months he's been dating Eunice. The boy often stays at her cousin's when she and Mark go out, or he'll be in bed when Mark comes over. And Eunice is so young herself, though she refers, rather dramatically, to a 'former life' before she knew who she was – before she 'found dance'. That's where Chad's from, the other life, as if he gave birth to her. This peculiar relationship contains a politics of equality that Mark didn't know and still doubts is possible between parents and their children; there's much language of *bargaining, balancing, reasoning* and *negotiating.* Yet one night, as they were enjoying a toke at her place and Chad's face appeared through the kitchen doorway, Eunice had snapped, 'Get back to bed, you little rat.' Mind you, she was pretty drunk.

Never has Eunice suggested that she's looking for a potential father for her son, and he's hardly a choice candidate. But then abruptly, today, she needs him to babysit. Last-minute audition, cousin busy – perhaps that's all it is. Or maybe it's just the beginning. First, the illusion of low maintenance, and then ...

So. Is he in love with her?

All right. In love with her enough?

Up ahead the Arthur Laing Bridge rises to cross the river. Mark exits and ramps up, leaving Marine Drive's strip malls and protective fences. At the arc's crest a diverse panorama appears: to the east lie crowded suburbs, while west and immediately south an undeveloped floodplain stretches to Vancouver airport and beyond to the ocean shore. Today's thick cloud-cover makes what could be an expansive place seem close, subdued.

The car's motor cuts out silently, though Mark senses the power loss though his body like a sudden drop. He's in the midst of a lane change and gets an irritated honk as the car loses speed. Veering onto the airport exit he tries to restart, the car becoming clumsy with its own weight until the engine catches and pulls them west.

'Bugger it!' Mark says, gearing up. Fucking shitbox car, fucking wasted day. First Eunice with her emergency, and then, just as he'd settled down Chad with a movie and got to his script, Allan calls. Mark takes a mouthful of warm coffee, glances at Chad and raises his voice over the music, some colourless techno downloaded by his roommate.

'How you doing back there, Chad? Good?'

The boy's Asiatic eyes shift briefly from the window. The eyes are slightly disturbing to Mark. Thick single lids, sharply tapering corners ... something reptilian there. On Eunice he finds them alluring, but not on the boy.

'Great,' Mark says. 'You just enjoy. This won't take long, and then we'll get back to your movie.' And to work, for fuck's sake.

Work. Here's an old but interesting question to ponder during the drive: who is Allan Petrynko? Mark still wants to put Allan Petrynko in a script, but has never been able to come up with the right angle on his character. Rural redneck or wise man of the woods? Reluctant hero or reluctant criminal? What do you do with an eco-activist, supporter of the NRA, large-scale dope farmer, the author of an anonymous pamphlet called *How Marijuana Farms Can Save Canada's Economy,* and possibly a Hell's Angel? That's Allan, Mark's dealer and the closest thing he's had to a boss for the last couple of years, the little he knows of him. For a long time Mark assumed Allan was American, but from a singular weekend at his farm, spent devastatingly stoned, he can recall an episode in the kitchen, time unknown, in which Allan, recounting his family's history in the Quebec townships, slammed his fist on the table and cried: 'That's it, you see? You fucking see?' All Mark can remember is something about a ranch, a hockey team, teenage pregnancy, ice.

At a T-junction Mark leaves the flow of airport traffic for a narrow, pitted road that heads north across the plain to a wall of bush, then turns west to parallel the airport road. Lying ahead to the southwest, the airport's buildings have become more distinct, and the long white cylinders of planes parked at terminals, yet all is still hazy and semi-substantial. Only the observation tower provides a vertical anchor.

What he can't entirely see Mark hears – and distinctly feels – despite the music: the long rising and falling notes of plane engines. A sign along the bush side of the road proclaiming this to be an 'Ecologically Sensitive Area' brings a snort of laughter from him.

The first house is a surprise. But then there's next one, and a next. Residents? Out here? On both sides of the road are old bungalows with lazy yards and even a couple of farm houses, leftovers from a bygone economy. Another plane rends the air. The houses facing the airport have their curtains drawn. Amazing, Mark thinks. Why don't they just give up and move to the runway?

Then he sees the horse.

Swift and sudden, the horse is moving alongside a wire fence that separates airport lands from scrub acreage. Without thinking Mark hits the brakes.

The animal is taller and bulkier than he remembers of horses, though it's been a very long time since he saw one this close. The broad back and haunches, the barrel belly, taper to such dainty, wrist-sized ankles. The rider is a woman in a white blouse and jeans. As another plane takes off the horse tosses its head, its mane streaming in the wind.

'Horsey!'

Chad starts prying at the slitted window.

'Yes, a strange horsey out here,' Mark says, reaching over to rummage in his knapsack for the camera he always keeps with him. An incoming plane has just rolled down a runway on the other side of the fence and the horse is right in front of it.

From the back seat Chad makes urgent grunting noises, followed by a mechanical click.

'Chad! *No.*'

Mark twists around to grab the unbuckled belt, then has to lean right over the seat, one foot still jammed precariously against the clutch as he holds the squirming boy down and re-secures the belt. Chad's pudgy hands immediately work at the buckle with a determination that starts a tug-of-war and ends with both of them red-faced, Chad wailing and tipping off the phone books, Mark sweating as he tightly grasps both boy and buckle, his blood throbbing with a sense of the infinite and terrifying exhaustions of parenthood.

'Chad, I'm sorry but we can't get out here,' he keeps saying. 'We have to go to the beach. The *beach*. You'll get to play by the water.' Probably not the right thing to say, he thinks, given that it's December. In fact, at close to three o'clock, the day is fast waning.

Mark grabs a Hershey bar from his knapsack and cracks it on the dashboard. He hands Chad an appeasingly large chunk. Then, still keeping one hand awkwardly pressed against the quieting child, he accelerates toward the beach. The horse and rider are quickly behind them.

5.

Mark wakes up. It's the winter of 1998 in Toronto, the time noon, the day Christmas. His Mom is in Florida. His roommates are out of town.

Draped in a sleeping bag, Mark makes a pot of coffee and a pile of pancakes pooled in cheap syrup, then settles himself on the living-room couch with his breakfast, a baggie of pot, rolling papers, a lighter, his notebook and pen, a razor blade, and a sachet of coke, a Christmas gift from his friend who runs the speakeasy he's been working at since the summer. Where his real education began, he sometimes thinks. On the floor by the TV stand is a stack of videos. He cuts into his pancakes.

Films fill his head day in and day out. Walking about the city, he thinks, What scene would play against this parking lot? What kind of person would buy that car? Whenever he meets anyone, he thinks, What kind of character is suggested by that voice? By those shoes? Potential: it's all about seeing it. He eavesdrops. He gets into situations.

Recently he made two decisions. One: to quit university. A

couple of his professors are cool and he's made a bunch of friends, but campus life is so tidy and exclusive it feels like a colonial compound. It's offensive and plain boring and above all, slow.

Two: to be a full-time screenwriter. That's what he should have been doing all along, only he didn't have the confidence yet, thought he needed the official education. He's written only two short scripts, but he knows absolutely that writing films is what he's meant to do. Films make his soul sing.

He dreams of being respected, sought after, imitated and inimitable. To get there he must always be focused, see everything. There are no dull moments – just wasted ones.

Except that it isn't true. There's plenty of dull, a numbing overabundance of it. If he could just be a film, art and life inseparable so all the dullness and repetition are trimmed away, leaving smooth sequencing. Movements from here, to here, to here.

Screenwriting's a total commitment, no 'second', practical career to lure him into thinking it's more important to own a dishwasher than to fulfill his heart's desire. If his scripts make having that stuff possible, fine. But he won't be sentenced to an office, wearing his mortgage face, to get it.

This fall, he started taking pictures. Using an old Polaroid camera he's collected shots of people, locations, odd urban details. At night, when he's not at the bar or watching videos, he spreads the photos under a lamp and arranges and rearranges them, making clusters, family trees. On the photos' white rims he's scribbled dates and key words of commentary:

• Zoë at Dean's: believes in telepathy. Reads Tarots
• Coleman's Deli employee: A Jewish Danny DeVito (or is he?). But tragic.
• Subway man. Lecturing loudly to woman/spouse re real estate prices in Bolton.
• Alley off Ossington. Hat bag with teddy bear inside.
• Bellwoods Park. Guy always wearing all-white clothes and always out when I am.
• T. J. from Detroit. Gun in pocket. Going to street race his Honda.

The most compelling shots he tapes into a thick, hard-backed notebook quickly filling up with script ideas and outlines.

Having finished his pancakes, Mark carries the plate into the kitchen, where he calls his mother. She's just heading out to a banquet in the complex but wants to know if he got the package she mailed.

'It arrived two days ago, Mom. Thanks a lot.'

'Nothing was damaged?'

'No, the clock is great. It's beside my bed. The oranges are sitting here in a bowl.' He rolls one onto the counter and picks it up. 'How are you?'

'Just fine. Don't let them sit too long, they're best fresh. Do the socks fit?'

'They're great.'

'Good. I've got to go right now, sweetie, but we'll talk soon. Lots of love.'

Throughout the day he watches *Fargo, Withnail and I, Desperado, The Good, the Bad and the Ugly, Slacker.* He smokes the dope, snorts the coke. He feels very happy. This week, he'll decide whether to spend the rest of his student loan on a one-year, unlimited Greyhound pass good for all of North America, or a 1974 Valiant for sale by a man named Dwayne who lives off Eastern Avenue (His photo is pasted into the script book: 'Dwayne: curiously obsessed with traffic accidents.').

In his notebook Mark writes, 'Great films are often about total losers. Film is the medium for transforming the narcissism and arrogance of the audience into compassion.'

Mark rereads the last sentence. Yes, he believes that. Every single adult in the world has a story to tell, a story of survival. And everyone, sufficiently prompted and encouraged, wants a listener. This is the narcissism, the vulnerable ego at the root of humanity. But everyone is also part of the audience, part listener. And under normal, social conditions, people suck at listening – they're too insecure, vain, distracted, incurious. Sit them in front of a screen, however, and something happens: they get interested in others.

He copies the sentence into a new section in the notebook, under

the title 'Thoughts on the Transformative Role of Film in Society'.
Maybe he'll write about this one day.

6.

At Iona Beach Mark is sitting on a damp driftwood log, his cell phone
hanging from one hand between joggling knees. The beach is utterly
empty. The ocean wind chills.

Allan hasn't shown or called. Attempts to contact him yielded
one connection that went –

(Static, car-tire whizz)

Yeah!

(silence)

Allan? It's Mark. I'm –

(Static) (silence) (static)

– so I've had – (static) – today – (tires) – don't –

(silence)

His hands are red and stiff. He mitts one and slaps the phone into
it again and again. Looks over his shoulder toward the small dirt parking lot, wishing for a concession stand. Hot coffee.

Chad, more protectively dressed by his mother in corduroys and
a bulky fleece jacket, is by the water. First he was pretending to be
chased by waves reaching up the beach, but now he's standing at the
edge of the waterline, watching planes. Just down the shore the planes
taking off shoot out from behind a stand of trees and over the water,
climbing slowly and heavily toward the clouds. In seconds the blinking tail lights vanish. Then, sometimes while a departed plane's
engines are still rumbling like receding thunder, a pair of white lights
will appear in the clouds: round, almost insect-like, they approach
silently, brightening until with a scream the incoming plane drops
down into view, flying so low it seems about to smash into the shoreline until it too slips behind the trees.

Great location, Mark thinks. Summer sunbathers under the
planes; that's weird. Postmodern public beach. The attractions of
noise – like those RV parks beside freeways. Excuse to crank your
stereos and TVs. Surround sound! Conversation in shouts. Scream

or shoot a gun and nobody can hear. He takes his Polaroid from his knapsack and gets a photo of a departing plane, writes a note on the bottom.

Another plane leaves the shore. Chad's body twists to track its ascent.

Mark checks the time again: 3:45. Already getting dark. Allan's erratic about his trips to Vancouver and Mark's reluctant to leave without at least talking to him. But Eunice will be through soon, and though Chad's been behaving, it'll be a relief to take him back.

Another pair of headlights. One could imagine that all these planes are really the same superfast jet returning in seconds. A mechanical bee-creature of the clouds, gathering, returning, gathering...

Mark rises and stomps sand from his boots. 'Chad! We're going.' He turns around. A blue sedan's pulling up to the parking lot. But Allan drives a truck.

The car stops behind the Honda, half-blocking it in, and a man gets out. He looks at the back of the Honda, maybe reading the licence plate, then raises his head and gazes toward Mark.

Mark thinks: Petrynko's been busted. But how would they know about the meeting?

Wiretaps. Holy fuck.

'Chad! Let's go. Now.'

As Mark heads toward the car, he reasons that the police could have no evidence on him. He and Allan keep their phone calls brief and neutral. Mark's own clients are all people he knows.

The man disappears into the washroom and emerges when Mark reaches the lot. He glances at the car: some cushy Chrysler model, but getting old. No one inside. The first three letters of the licence plate – LAT – jump out at him. LATT.

'Hello there,' the man says. He's in his fifties or sixties, nylon windbreaker and small, faraway eyes behind glasses too large for his face. Perhaps a birdwatcher? In December?

With a nod Mark opens the driver's door. From the other side of the car the man says, 'Your back right's getting low.'

'What's that?'

'Your back right.'

Mark reluctantly walks around and looks. Sure enough, the bottom of the tire bulges noticeably. 'Oh yeah,' he says. 'Thanks.'

'Do you have a spare? I can help you out.'

'A spare? It doesn't look that bad.'

The man shrugs, seems a bit disappointed.

Mark walks back to the driver's side.

'Sure gets dark early,' the man says, watching a plane disappear. 'Pretty lousy day to come to the beach.'

'Yeah. We're just leaving, actually. Do you mind moving your car?'

'Sure.' He moves off slowly. Retired, Mark thinks. Bored and lonely.

The ring of the phone startles him. 'Hello? Allan! Where the fuck –' Stepping toward the washrooms, he turns his back so the man will take the hint. Through static Allan relays that he's been towed to a service station near Mission. Mark plugs his other ear to listen. The sound of a plane taking off moves through his head.

A minute later he snaps the phone shut and turns to see the sedan disappearing up the road.

'Chad! Let's go.'

But Chad isn't there.

Mark looks around the car. Inside it. He calls out. The first pang of dread touches him, but then he remembers the washrooms. Of course! He enters the men's, then the women's, where clean concrete stalls sit empty and the wind whistles in through high, slatted windows. Outside again, Mark circles the washrooms and shouts over and over. He threatens. He runs up the beach until his chest hurts, calling. Think back, Mark: where was the boy last? You saw him wandering around the parking lot with a stick, while you were talking to the man with the sedan.

The man.

Mark clutches at his shirt. The man's car has vanished. It's maybe six, seven minutes to the highway – or the airport – and several have been wasted already. There are those bungalows on the road, too. But it's impossible, he was only turned away for a moment! Chad must be hiding. Or he's just run off. Children are absent-minded, they misplace themselves like kittens – don't they? Mark looks up the beach: it runs the edge of a point of land that stretches perhaps a kilometre into the ocean, scruffy and barren-looking despite another sign pertly proclaiming its ecological importance. But there's enough scrub foliage to hide a small boy.

'Jesus Christ, Jesus Christ!' Mark mutters over and over, frantically turning around. As a last effort he dashes up the beach again and screams for Chad, then runs back to the car and floors it out of the lot. When he nears the houses he halves his speed and checks for the blue sedan. As if a child snatcher would park it in the driveway! Mark accelerates toward the airport road, scanning ahead. There's a dark car near the T-junction, turning left toward the bridge. He'll never catch up. He *will* catch up. He'll sideswipe the fucker.

What if Chad really has been hiding, though, and goes too close to the water? What if he's there now and someone else drives up?

He takes the bend toward the junction too fast and the wheels jump coming out of the turn. The engine cuts out.

Stalled at the T-junction, Mark starts crying. Tears sting and blur. He wipes his eyes and cannot find the man's car in all this traffic. Out over the plain arcs the great bridge, with vehicles rushing onto it from the airport road and merging with rush-hour traffic. Another plane takes off, another lands, people coming and going by the hundreds before he can restart the car and make his way back to the beach.

7.

Mark wakes up. He's lying under a blanket on a pad of yellow foam, with his wool sweater itching his cheek. On the floor are a pair of men's underwear and a bent ticket with a time printed on it. He rolls over and stares up at a ceiling so altered by bursts of fallen plaster, yellow smoke stains, blistering paint and sprays of black mould that it's become beautiful.

His underwear, his ticket.

It's a soggy afternoon in the spring of 2002. He's flown to London on a stand-by. He's here. One continent, one ocean, twelve hours from LATT.

After dressing, he finds the kitchen and joins two men and a woman sitting around the table with mugs of coffee, a toaster, a loaf of bread, a dirty ashtray, and a jar of jam impaled by a butcher's knife. One of the men is Sam, a friend who came over from LA last year and found under-the-table work at a club that Mark's going to work at too. The woman is an Australian and seems to be Sam's lover. The other man is named Allan Petrynko.

By October Mark has paid off his personal debts and is just starting to save money when business falls off at the club and his hours are cut. Just as well, because he's developing tinnitus.

London is a mystery. The sophisticated debauchery of the club is familiar enough from LA. He's met lawyers, criminals, athletes, models, executives, entertainers and countless idiots. Briefly, he's dated a German video artist and an English medical student who slept in her bra and panties. But though he's taken many photos and written up his experiences, it's always been with the feeling that he's observing through layers of incomprehension – years thick, at least. It's like missing part of a sentence, over and over. And it's not just the accents, the different cultural references. The Old World just isn't his milieu.

LA was different, but things got fucked up. Before he left he thought his head would explode: three years as an on-again/off-again courier, in the end living on-again/off-again at a hacienda-style house with a woman who 'liked artists' and didn't charge rent so long as he occasionally slept in her bed (Try Anything Once). Working to meet the right people and meeting their friends instead, their Pilates instructors, their ex-lovers and coke suppliers but never the *right people*. Well, not quite. There were some almosts: twice, a script of his came close to being optioned. Perhaps he'll make some calls to LA. Or Seattle. He has friends there.

Canada's been a problem since he defaulted on his student loan.

One night when Sam's out working, Allan Petrynko calls from

BC. Mark and Allan end up talking for forty minutes. Allan says, People change names all the time. No one checks.

When Mark leaves England it's a sunny day, noon. Over the mid-Atlantic the sky pales then brightens like they've crossed a wrinkle. He lands at Pearson Airport just past noon. Transfers. Is up in the air again by two. As they're crossing Lake Superior he falls asleep and wakes up to a stewardess's slight cleavage. The face above it is saying 'Sir. Sir. We've landed.'

'Who?' he says.

'Sir. We've landed in Vancouver.'

He looks out the window. He can see the ocean.

8.

In a way it's tidy. The police find Chad before midnight. An officer at the station says they spotted the boy wandering near the road, a couple of kilometres from the beach.

Earlier at her apartment, while they waited for news, Eunice sat alone and almost motionless, hugging herself. To Mark she became unrecognizable; nowhere in this person could he discern the woman who called Chad a 'little rat'. At first, when she'd simply been hysterical, he'd sensed a role for himself and tried to be optimistic. Then when the police called and he said 'Thank God,' she hit him on the chest with her fist. Careless. You're so fucking careless

She won't stand with him at the station. Chad arrives, carried in the arms of a policeman. The boy's clearly in shock. One cheek of his glassy-eyed face bears an ugly red scrape, five or six thin, straight lines. He's also filthy: long smudges of grime on his pants suggest sliding, or dragging. There's a smell of urine. Eunice snatches him and begins to sob, sinking to her knees holding the boy, her long black hair falling over his head like a veil. Moved, the officers encircle them. One bends and places a hand on Eunice's shoulder, the other on Chad's back, and bows his head.

When it's over Mark drives them home. The car, at least, doesn't stall.

* * *

So there it is, end of story. Fade to black and roll credits. No animals were harmed during this production. As for persons, the doctor's report stated there appeared to be only superficial harm.

9.

Chad is lying somewhere, his eyes staring. Perhaps he's fallen down a ditch. Maybe he's been thrown down.

Chad is running across a stony surface. In the distance are moving lights. His winter clothes, his small pudgy limbs make him awkward. He trips and falls, scraping his face.

Here's Chad with his arm stuck out in front of him – caught inside a fist. His coat gets all bunched as he wriggles and tugs. Then a big hand comes down across his cheek and knocks the image away.

There is a plane, a horse. Mark sees Chad running across the beach. It's confusing. The composition keeps dissolving and reassembling. Occasionally there's a feeling – a wet, chilled, terribly uncomfortable feeling that surges up from the deep, and a sense of being peeled open to it, slowly filled up. Whenever the feeling comes Mark crosses his legs and hugs himself.

It's 2005 and Mark's back in LA, one optioned script under his belt and many more in a cardboard box in his rented room. When he's not helping his roommate with her catering business to pay his share of the rent, he goes to parties, he cold-calls strangers and name-drops. Selling a script is like coaxing a mouse through a maze. After weeks of anxious, trial-and-error activity, the mouse has progressed to an agent who's agreed to represent it. But that's not the end. The route from the agent to the final exit, the desk of a director, seems even harder, the way fractured into thousands of possibilities: there are false leads, strategic changes, and the odd shortcut. Updates from the agent change so often that the messages blur into a kind of constant, a cardiogram line rising and falling.

Yet the ring of the phone is still a jolt of adrenaline. As long as it does ring, Mark thinks, then things are good, despite his fatigue. It's there – the fatigue. A low-level, electrical buzzing in his arms and legs and fingers, worse behind his eyes. His concession to it was to see a doctor and to follow half of his advice: Quit coffee? Not on your life! Take up exercise? Perhaps a good idea. And so he's started running, and has become addicted. Aside from driving it seems the perfect activity for LA. The runners are in a smaller league than the motorists. Elite. There's a contact that he loves: a peripheral flick with the eyes, part greeting, part mutual admiration, when two runners pass.

One weekday afternoon Mark's out running along the Venice Beach boardwalk toward Santa Monica, where he lives. Over the ocean hovers a tepid October sun, flat and pale. The first two kilometres of his route are the hardest; there's nausea and head pain, and his limbs feel heavy. But once his body warms up it accepts the speed. Then he feels like he can go forever.

The path's crowded today, knotted at access points with dog walkers and kids he wants to plow aside like bowling pins. There should be a freeway for us, he thinks. A separate network.

As he runs Mark tries to stay in the moment and not think about the room he must return to. You don't need much to survive. He found his index card holder in a garbage bin. Hardcover notebooks are $1.50 in Chinatown and cheaper if you bargain for a bulk rate. Tuna is usually on sale. He's good to set up his laptop on any flat surface so long as it's clean: kitchen table, coffee table, bed, and once, when he owned none of these, on a stack of milk crates covered with newspaper.

When he sees the end point of his run he breaks into a sprint, then finishes bent double, hands on his knees. A minute later he straightens, checks his cell phone. The agent has called: a 'down' week.

He thinks: I'll give her one more month.

Above him a jet crosses the sky, leaving a white trail of smoke that intersects with another left minutes before. He watches the plane then walks on, wiping his face with his shirt. One cannot care about mistakes. If he can just go forward, just reach what he wants. Live in a time zone of his own making.

Before entering his house he pauses on the sidewalk, eyes closed, and welcomes the motion of whizzing traffic like a cool breeze.

Ship of Fools

A friend once told me I have a look that attracts lost souls. 'Sanity' is how she described it. 'You have the gleam of sanity in your eyes.'

Surely that's true of most people? Not like you, she said.

This friend was fond of making pronouncements that she refused to explain. Doled out insights, or the promise of them, like coins dropped from a passing carriage. At my job, though, it's not a question of attracting. I'm behind the counter, with the power. They're on the other side, with their dreadfully plain needs. Neither of us can walk away.

When Celia calls I'm filling out a check-in form for an eager young woman with a fun-fur jacket that's dripping wet. I've seen her once before, only this time she's got more drugs in her and a smeary bruise under one blue eye. She says her name's Jennifer, but spells it wrong.

'New Hope,' I say.

'Um, can I please speak to Hannah?'

'Speaking. Oh hi, Celia.' My pen stops. This is it, I think: doom. Someone has died. The house has exploded. Celia, my roommate, never calls me at work. We don't have that kind of sisterly relationship, one that could inspire the making of a real home instead of the transitional space we live in. It became clear after I moved in that we were a disappointment to each other. But we try, we maintain good appearances, share occasional meals and personal stories in a kind of homage to a more ideal friendship.

Celia speaks with her usual warm, somewhat distracted tone, as if she's enjoying a foot massage. 'Oh! Hi,' she says. 'I didn't recognize your voice there. How are you? I hope it's okay that I'm calling you at work?'

I relax and resume writing. I've got to get a handle on this panic thing.

The reception desk has a counter attached to the front, which I like to stand up and use so clients can watch what I'm doing. The transparency principle: very important around here. Swaying a little on the other side of the counter and gripping it with blunt fingers is Jennifer, who seems fascinated by my pen.

'How's it going there?' Celia asks.

'Fine.'

There's a hurt silence over the line. 'I'm just in the middle of seeing someone,' I explain. 'What's up?'

Celia sympathizes. 'Oh I know, you must be so busy. Unfortunately, eh? I just have a quick question. Do you know what Rashinga Mountain is?'

'What?' I repeat the name aloud.

'Rasha,' Jennifer says with a giggle. She gives me an excited look. Up for anything, it says. Anything.

Celia spells out the name, then tells me about the package.

'Sounds like a spiritual retreat, a yoga centre. Is there a return address?

Crinkling sounds over the receiver. 'Um, it says Hornby Island.'

'Okay, so we'll send it back.'

'How do we do that?'

This simple question floors me. Though she has a pharmacopoeia of herbal lore in her head and is the assistant manager of a non-profit agency, Celia often doesn't know the most basic things. As I'm explaining the concept of return post and saying goodbye, Jennifer leaves the counter, lopes across the empty reception room on long, veiny legs and scuffed heels, and goes awkwardly out the glass doors to the sidewalk. A man's standing there. Jennifer waves at me merrily as they leave.

I put the check-in form aside. For some moments, the New Hope Shelter and Help Centre reception area is peaceful. Spinning slowly in my chair, I listen to the rain and stare at the false ceiling, where there's a water stain shaped like a pine tree.

Rashinga Mountain?

Two days later I meet the real thing. Not an it – a he.

* * *

After work I often head over to a West End café where I can see the beach and eat something incredibly healthy, a sprouts and organic greens salad, a fresh-squeezed juice blend of carrot, ginger and apple. Gazing at the bay and robust faces around me I feel a settling inside, the world returning to even keel.

But because it's Friday and I have plans tonight I cycle home directly – just in time, it turns out, to avert certain disaster. In the lane beside our house I weave through the kids from the Chinese restaurant playing ball hockey, and when I come around back I see Celia standing at the door. Talking to her is an anaemic-looking hippie with a duffle bag at his feet.

'Here's Hannah,' Celia announces as I mount the steps to the rattletrap porch off our entrance. She seems hesitant, but this is often how she looks, a side effect, I think, of her constant striving to remain 'non-judgmental'. Her skin's so clear from the herb regimen that it shines; I imagine her colon as a dewy pod, her poop the finest loam. 'Hannah,' she says, 'this is Rashinga. The package came for him!' She smiles as if all mysteries are now explained.

'Rash,' says the hippie with the borrowed name, making room for me on the porch and extending a pale hand.

'Nice to meet you. Did you get the envelope?' With a little sound Celia disappears into the house, leaving me to stare harder than usual at this stranger who's receiving mail at our address and knows it. Rash blinks at me with languid eyes. Atop his head looms a bulge of hair, presumably dreads, collected under a woollen-knit cap.

'So …' I prompt.

Rash picks it up. 'Yeah, as I was telling Celia, I just got into town and came over to see June.'

'June? She's been in Guatemala for over a year.'

'Yeah, that's what Celia told me. She probably wrote me but I've been moving around a lot. Sometimes I can't go back and get my mail.'

'You used to live here?'

'Ah, no. It's an address.'

Celia reappears with the package, a large, padded envelope. With a glance at the return address Rash shoves it in his bag. He has an odd manner, a ganja sedateness broken by sure, masculine movements that speak of latent energies. I can tell Celia's also disappointed that he didn't open the envelope here. The thing weighs like a textbook but is squishy, the paper plastered with an expensive row of stamps.

'So June let you receive mail here?'

'Yeah, as I was saying to Celia' – he gives her a respectful nod, like she's a *lady* or something – 'this was kinda my crash place in Vancouver. You know June?'

I explain that I arrived to live here after June left and Celia had moved in. June is Celia's friend (a sisterly one).

'Cool,' Rash says, regarding me like I'm one of the honoured ones too, those associated with the saintly June, who's now fending off mosquitoes and drunken soldiers as she heads up a business development project for women in a jungle-edged town.

'We'll give you her address, if you'd like.'

'Sure. That would be great,' he says, still wearing that awed expression, and I realize this is his Look: a sort of innocent reverence toward everything. Probably based on some world-in-a-grain-of-sand principle, a Buddhist-cum-communist, tread-gently approach that's as artificial as his patchouli reek and ridiculous globalism (Indian name, Rastafarian hair, and I'd bet on a medley of piercings and tattoos beneath those fibrous clothes).

I ask Rash if he's expecting more mail. Oh maybe, maybe not, is that okay with us? Sure, Rash. My stomach's grumbling. Celia brings June's address on a slip of paper. 'Well, see you later,' I say, and step toward the door, which Celia is blocking. She gives me a stricken look and doesn't budge.

'Rash,' she asks, 'do you have somewhere else to stay?'

Somewhere *else*?

His eyes go flicker-flicker from Celia to me. The duffle bag is suddenly shrill. 'Uh, maybe,' he says. 'I know some people … I haven't been in Vancouver for a while. As I said, June's place was always open, you know? Bodies all over the floor.' When Celia's head starts turning my way I catch her meaning perfectly and go into full alert.

'Sorry, Rash, but I'm not comfortable having a stranger stay here.' I'm now squeezed into the doorframe beside Celia, whose body's emitting high-frequency vibrations of social anxiety. For me, this is just work.

'I'm sure you can appreciate that in a house of two women, we have to be careful,' I explain. 'And it's not like June ever mentioned you to us.'

'Oh sure, sure.' Rash thumbs his scruffy beard. After an awkward silence, he snaps out of his daze and hoists his bag.

'Well, thanks for the mail. Nice to meet you,' he adds, glancing at Celia hopefully, then at me like a dog that's been told to shoo. He starts down the steps.

'Oh, you're *welcome*, Rash.' Celia's got her sympathy voice going, a coddling vibrato. 'Come back and leave us a number, okay? In case we get anything else.'

I'm already inside, this last bit heard as I open the refrigerator, select some cheese and a malty, Belgian beer. In the living room I toss my knapsack and helmet on the couch, flop down and enjoy my first tangy sip. We've got a dumpster view, rotted window frames and walls begging for paint and plaster that neither of us is inspired to buy; still, our apartment offers refuge. My plants are rowed along the sill, cheerfully unfurling new leaves. Thank God I came home! A quarter hour more and Rash would have colonized this room. I can see his possessions on the floor (a notebook bound with an elastic, rolling tobacco, woven dope pouch and a blanket of some archaic wool). I can feel him, here like a spreading spill.

Celia takes a while coming in. I'm ready for her when she does.

'I know that seemed abrupt,' I say as she sits herself on the opposite sofa, 'but the guy's a total stranger and he was being pretty abrupt himself, arriving and expecting a bed.'

'I know.' She sighs. The poor thing's wilted with remorse: shoulders slumped, her large breasts dolefully low.

I raise my eyebrows at her.

'It still seemed a little mean,' she says. 'Considering.'

'Considering?'

'That he's a friend of June's. And he's probably fine.'

'I suppose. But I was being careful.'

This Celia nods to because she knows all about the dangers of men. Ironically, she's usually the cautious one, nervous of night walks from the bus stop, of men with stylish haircuts and cars. But a gentle hippie is something else – like one of the family, which for Celia is a loose coalition of supposed anti-establishment comrades who meet with her approval: health-food-store customers and employees, environmentalists and other left-wing agitators, single mothers, poor mothers and poor women, women of colour and lesbians, meekly destitute men, meekly non-white men, gay men and persons who have changed their sex.

'Personally,' I continue, 'I resent guests who arrive at the door unannounced and assume you'll drop everything for them. A good friend is one thing, but a stranger? It's ... *disrespectful*.'

This argument works on her like a buttress of reason and good sense. Her expression firms up.

'You're right.'

'And did you notice how he never mentioned how long he needed to stay? What's that about? Do you want a beer?'

She shakes her head. I pick up my paper from the captain's chest that's our coffee table, thinking that's the end of it.

That night I'm out late downtown with a friend, a gay man I work with who's also single and prefers, as I do, the chatty atmosphere of a crowded pub to the poser scene of the bars. After we close the Railway Club and say goodbye I pitch through the rain searching for a cab, finally veering to the Hastings Street bus stop. I'm drunk enough that the cold rain feels delicious on my skin. In the bus headlights it looks like falling needles.

Boarding is a shock. At this hour the bus is a stifling capsule of dank bodies, like the interior of a single, slowly digesting organism. I squeeze through the bibulous crowd, spot two empty seats in the far back corner and nab one. At the next stop the crowd shuffles, then a belligerent voice rises. Above people's heads appears an enormous and violently drunk man, advancing toward the back like a boulder. He has great pudgy cheeks with eyes like pinched buttons and he makes right for me, for that lone seat. In my awe I don't scoot fast enough and he lands beside me with a sulphurous FUCK! The bus whines forward.

Jammed against the window, I get the full effect of every rattle and jolt as we hurtle east, a strange carnival of souls on wheels, a ship of fools. No one is sober or bright-eyed here, at this hour. The young are old, the old like wraiths. We've all come from doing things to our bodies that we'd be better off not doing, and God knows what's next. Rain runs down the windows so the world outside is a phantom scene of lights and gloom.

Once, mildly drunk, I made the mistake of dropping into the shelter during one of my after-the-bar lags home. This wasn't long after I stopped working the weekend night shift, but my friend was still doing it for another few weeks; we were hired at the same time, learned the ropes together and became friends that way. That night, my drinking companions gone, I decided to visit my friend and taunt him a little with my newfound freedom.

I walked into the usual weekend pandemonium: dishevelled people were slouching or lying on the chairs, the floor, each other. If the Hastings Street bus is the ship of fools, the New Hope reception room on weekend nights is that ship washed up and wrecked – an emergency ward of peasants strewn about our bolted-down chairs, a damaged and beggarly lot, a hacking, malnourished crew. Marred with cuts, blue with bruises, bitten by disease: HIV, hep B, TB and a host of lesser discomforts, the gals with their itchy yeast infections, the guys with painful pee ... their minds agitated by chemical visions, by vitamin deficiencies, by booze and prescription psychotropics and the countless free coffees with sugar cubes consumed in the waiting room and always, like a strong current, by those memories and dreams that urged them here from their uncertain origins.

The architecture and décor of the reception room, which I'd experienced only when sober, now struck me as disdainfully institutional, a school classroom. And I was never a contented student ...

The officious desk and fluorescent lighting, the orderly chairs and brochure racks – what a feeble pose of know-how. How could I blame anyone for misbehaving? I too wanted to gab about life and lie on the floor. Lighten up, dudes! My friend was sweating behind the counter and when I smirked and waved he gave me a puzzled scowl. Chastened, I slunk away. In the morning I felt like I'd done something slightly obscene. Things between my friend and me were awkward for a while after that.

When I reach home from the bus stop (after having to wake Sumo to leave my seat; he roared and brandished a fat fist like an oversized baby) an even weirder scene greets me. Our back porch is glowing from what appears to be a fire. A figure is huddled over it.

I mount the steps slowly. 'Rash?'

'Oh. Hi.' He looks sheepish, but not nearly as much as one would expect. Sure enough, draped over his shoulders is a colourful Indian blanket, while at his feet is a camping stove on which a covered pot's steaming.

'Rash, what are you doing here?'

He removes the lid and begins stirring the dark and grainy contents. 'Yeah, well, my other place fell through, but I didn't know till late. So I came here and thought I'd set up my tent in your yard, but it started raining.' Water's pelting the porch's corrugated-plastic roof, pouring over its edges in hypnotically regular streams.

Rash has spread a sleeping bag between my reading chair and the recycling boxes we store out here. Though the porch floor's dry, the scene's still pathetic. A voice inside me says it's inhuman to let Rash sleep out here on a wet night while I lie close by, snug in bed. Yet the air's warm enough, and his lapsing back here like a stray is just the kind of manipulativeness I loathe. What about his friend's yard?

'Do you want some wheat berries?'

'No thanks. Rash, do you need a blanket or pillow or something?'

'No, I'm great here. Got everything. You sure you don't want some berries? They're really good?'

'Go ahead. I'm, uh, I'm really beat. Good night.'

I lie awake under the duvet for a while, wondering if Rash might burn the place down with his stove. The house is covered in cedar shingles painted a faded, ugly pink. But it's a wet night; it's more likely he'll catch pneumonia, chilblains. There's a fine layer of guilt around my heart about this. Admittedly I don't think Rash is dangerous, but he irritates. He *affronts*. Just because I work in a shelter doesn't mean I should run one at home. I mean, no one wants to live in one, 'bodies all over the floor'. And Rash isn't like our clients: he's healthy and calm, he has lots of friends; his apparent poverty is a lifestyle choice based on political-spiritual principles. Some people say that about the addicts and prostitutes and other ne'er-do-wells who use New Hope, but I know choice vanished from their lives a long time ago, slipped through the walls with the future and the past.

I listen to the rain. No, there's no irony to me.

By the time I'm up the next morning Rash is gone and so is Celia. At dinnertime I ask her if she's seen him. I'm not sure she even knows he was here.

'He was still there this morning,' she replies. She's mincing garlic and I note that yesterday's firmness has given way to the cloistered manner she gets when wounded: eyes averted, lips a grim line. One complication in our household arrangement is that Celia doesn't like me. I believe she mostly wills herself to be friendly out of ideological reasons (i.e., my job, which she admires) and because I'm a good roommate. Secretly, she's haunted by darker feelings. And why not? She certainly bothers me: she's lazy around the house, she's naïve, she believes in being tolerant and unprejudiced and calls this an alternative lifestyle, yet it's really just reverse prejudice against anyone who's middle class – really just her own inherited middle-class righteousness in banal new form. Of course I have the same heredity. It does cause problems.

Watching her dice burdock root for her 'tuber stew' recipe, I consider the meaning of her answer. Obviously she knew that Rash was outside, so they must have spoken last night. And this morning, was he sleeping? Getting high? Or was there further conversation?

'Did he say anything about coming back?'

Celia hesitates. 'I think he's going to look for another place to stay,' she says. Which is not really answering the question, but her manner is so tight that I drop the subject.

Coming home that night I ride up the lane with dread, but the porch is dark and no unusual forms disrupt the yard's grassy expanse. So Rash has found a spare couch or sod patch, and I can stop feeling like I've behaved badly. I don't really believe I have, but Celia's mute disapproval has a way of working on me. I'm an easy target for guilt, what with my sugar-coated upbringing and my job helping our clients, many of them Natives whose ruin was sowed so diligently by those successful ancestors of mine.

Here's how it is at work:

The person across the counter from me, whom I'm trying to 'help', is a boy of twenty-three. He lives on and presumably works the streets, has a murky sexual orientation, likely uses drugs, and is HIV positive. He also has some kind of organic or induced mental health problem: poor attention span, cognitive skills so limited that, like a small child, he has trouble understanding what I mean by 'five hours from now'. I point to a clock. 'When the big hand gets to six …'

'Ow,' he keeps saying, one hand reaching behind him to tug at the butt of his shorts.

Abruptly he announces: 'I got anal herpes.' This is not a confession. His eyes never lock focus.

Later there's a man, soft-spoken, thick glasses, dark pitted skin. He's finally gotten into subsidized housing and he needs a couch. Every week he comes here to ask if we can do something. We're not in the furniture business, but we're in the help business, so he asks. One day he starts and will not stop telling me what was done to him by his stepfather. From between his swollen lips a blackness emerges to press against me. It slips inside. I feel rancid, worthless. I want to crawl under the desk.

'That's terrible,' I mumble.

That's …

But the day improves. At lunch a colleague tells me that a client whom we spent months working with to get into rehab and then an apartment has just overdosed. I give her a eureka look and we say it together: 'She's got a couch!'

'Get the fucking couch!'

'The couch! The couch!' I cry, laughing, running down the hall to start making calls.

It's not like I don't agree with Celia's middle-class critiques, but I've come to a new appreciation of the suburbs.

Monday morning there are two staff out front, four doing intake in the back and a handful of refugees in the waiting area. To avoid having to replace our receptionists all the time, we rotate the exhausting front-desk positions. I come out from the offices after lunch and pick up the clipboard containing the sign-up sheet we now use instead of a more bureaucratic number system.

'Shawn?'

I look over at a sinewy tranny wearing a pretty summer dress. She's sitting demurely with her legs crossed, a crusty gash down one arm that looks like it should have been stitched. As I'm considering whether I should get the first aid kit, a boy appears at the desk. He's so small and dark I hadn't noticed him sitting on the other side of the room, though now that he's in front of me I'm struck by his beauty. Not something we see much of.

'You're Shawn?' I smile right into his eyes, as I do with all clients. People like to know you're not afraid to take a genuine look at them; it calms them down, usually.

'Yes.' Not 'yeah' or some smart remark. Behind him in the waiting room, the tranny has begun to talk to a guy wearing an oversized nylon jacket.

'You need a place to stay? Have you been here before?'

Shawn shakes his head. He looks like he could be in high school but is probably in his early twenties. Tan, blemish-free skin. Perhaps he just left the reserve.

'Okay, I'll just get a quick bit of information on you.' I write his first name on the intake form, today's date, check the box alongside the shelter option. As I write, I can see peripherally that Shawn's staring at my face, and when I meet his eyes again there's a jolt of sexuality, like our bodies have exuded scent.

I don't miss a beat. 'We do have beds for tonight. You don't have to give me your real last name if you don't want to, just to have a bed. I've already put you down for one. But if you'd like some help with housing, or work, or something else, we'll need to know who you are.'

Our eyes rest on each other's. Shawn's are black, bottomless wells. They have a disturbing, infantile openness, like anything could reach or fall right in. They say two things: you have total power, and you have none. Is this a Look? Perhaps for johns? The face around the eyes, despite its delicate features, is rigid. Too much experience there, too much survival too young.

He shrugs. 'I can give my real name.'

'Do you want to see a counsellor too?'

'What could I see them about?' His eyes flick down to my chest and up again, continuing to watch closely.

'Well, there's getting some real housing, for starters. Employment. Health care, rehab, uh, whatever. There's also getting connected to some other groups, if you're new in town. A lot of young people' – I say this to dispel the erotic fug, this false intimacy I'm feeling – 'like meeting up with the folks at the Aboriginal Friendship Centre.'

'I don't want to see *them*,' Shawn says.

'Okay, just a bed for now.'

I bend over the form, sign it. The tranny and her friend are laughing, and the wholesomeness of the sound makes me smile. It's a good day: beautiful boy not yet wasted, happy clients. I reach for a brochure. 'If you change your mind,' I tell Shawn, 'or need to come back another time, here's a list of some things we can help you with.'

'Could I see you?'

'Sure,' I say, eager for the fascination of those eyes. At the same time I'm absurdly aware that kids don't learn to manipulate every situation sexually unless they need to. And few twenty-year-old boys are drawn to women pushing forty.

'My name's Hannah. But I'm not always on intake. Just some days.'

'Tomorrow?'

'Uh, yes.'

As he turns to go, Shawn gives me a grin that makes his toughness vanish, or seems to. The kid knows his talent: I'm as obvious as a reflection.

I pick up the clipboard. 'Angelica?'

The tranny strides to the counter and stands towering like some fairytale creature with her broadsword slash. 'How you doing, honey?' she asks.

'That's some knock,' I say.

Guess who's having a chat when I ride by? I see them as I'm turning onto our street, but they don't see me. They're standing by the apple bins in front of the Circling Dawn, an organic grocery and local hippie mecca.

I half expect to see the duffle bag on the porch again as I trudge up the rotting steps. What could they be talking about? Did they run into each other or meet on purpose? What purpose? And why do I care?

The black-haired heads of the Chinese restaurant kids bob past the living room window. A little hockey before sundown. I slump on the couch with another variety of extra-strong and expensive Belgian abbey beer. I keep a little cellar for myself, a habit that I know makes Celia uncomfortable for hazy moral reasons, probably to do with luxury. In another century she'd be a nun, an abbess herself. She doesn't think much of men (me, I think about men lots – particularly their absence from my life). And guys don't exactly bust the door down to go out with her – a fact that could be related to her dislike of men, but would be cruel to postulate as its direct cause. Abbess? Rather stern, but it fits. With a wimple, a gown like a tent.

Amusing myself like this, I finish the beer and pop another. I sit relishing its fizzy slide down my throat, the relaxing serum in my veins. The bottle empties. With a sigh, I look out the window. First-stage intoxication feels like two warm arms around me, and I never want it to stop.

Do I drink too much? When I first started working at New Hope five years ago I'd fall into bed by nine. I needed ten hours' sleep a night to deal with the stress. Gradually, with time and regular exercise, the stress receded. Or has become so pervasive I can't see it. True enough, returning to work after a vacation is like being hit by a truck, but I don't feel burnt out, my gay friend and I discuss this issue often and I really don't. It's more like at this point I don't know what else to do. Many things come to mind, but none beckon. I used to believe my work was about helping reduce suffering in the world; I was a soldier in the army of salvation. It seemed like the only worthwhile thing to do with my life. As a youth I was a green-haired punk for a while, a real one, running wild, indulging in hating the world for its evil. And before this nihilistic phase took hold was my first phase of salvationism: I was the little girl who donated her birthday money to Feed the Children and drove her mother crazy by taping up refugee camp pictures in my room. I can only swing between hope and hatred, it seems.

I wiggle my empty bottle, jump up and grab another from the fridge, but I get some food too, some almonds, black olives, goat cheese and crackers. I'll strive for balance in nutrition, at least.

Granville Street is crowded with versions of my punker self. I meet these kids' eyes. I too once touched the dark extreme – not for long, but a few months during those blurry days, months of so much drugs and sex and chaos that I started to forget about any other way to live. There is something ... there *is* something liberating, even purifying, about letting everything go. A strange new kind of childhood. It doesn't matter that you've been pushed and pulled there; driving forces are always present. What matters is that you finally say fuck it and let go of the reins. Drift along, like Jennifer.

Someone stomping up the back steps. I've left the door open, and twist around to look through the kitchen. In comes Celia carrying a load of groceries, followed by Rash, who's got his duffle bag in tow. I see it all that second, the whole conspiracy.

'Oh. Hi, Hannah,' Celia says, stopping. Standing straight, her thick legs like tree trunks and her breasts bountiful under a thin cotton blouse, she shines down on me, a Nordic matriarch. She nods toward Rash. She's got this prepared.

'I've invited Rash for dinner. We'll be having enchiladas, if you want some.'

'Hi, Hannah,' Rash says, with that obsequious nod.

'Hi Rash,' I reply, restraining a smirk. To Celia I say, 'That sounds nice.'

Yeah, I'm cool. Show me up as an asshole. No rise here.

It's a charming dinner, though all the while I'm wishing I'd had the forethought to lie and say I had plans. And I'm wondering how long Rash will be lodged here. Now that he's been presented as Celia's 'friend' I cannot, of course, make demands until propriety has been breached. A few days' stay has always been acceptable here for friends from out of town; I even had my sister for two weeks.

I try to get Rash to talk politics or religion, but overall he's not a very interesting hippie, not even a good storyteller or musician or physics Ph.D. dropout. He waves a placard at logging protests, he helps on an organic farm. He's not on welfare.

'So how *do* you live?' I ask, thrusting the bowl of avocado salad his way.

'Wheat berries.' He reaches into his duffle bag and brings out a depleted burlap sack. 'They're full of protein.'

'But that can't be all you eat.'

'Pretty well,' he says, with a spark that might be pride in those limpid eyes. 'I can live on a hundred dollars a month.'

Celia and Rash drink tea after supper while I retire to the living room with another beer to read and eavesdrop. With me Rash was guarded, I realize. He and Celia talk easily, and he actually does tell some colourful tales about living up in trees at Clayoquot Sound. He reveals some knowledge of herbs, too – impressive to Celia, of course. No, Rash was resisting me, treating me like a parent.

When Celia's made up a bed for Rash on the other couch and he's using the shower, we gals have a chat. Celia initiates it; I'm not saying anything until she does, though really it's hard to tell who's the wounded party. I believe I must be, but I know that from Celia's perspective, I 'started' it all, acted ungenerously by refusing to let a ragamuffin take over our place and by subjecting him to practical life questions at supper. She's just rectifying my meanness, restoring the karma.

Celia sits on Rash's couch with a book that she's been reading for about six months. She glances around furtively, gets up to check the palm tree for signs of spider-mite invasion, mists it down with soapy water, sits again. Fear of confrontation's got the poor thing jumpy. Plus, we're women: in her view, we should be sticking together. Getting divided over a man is alarming.

'I'm glad you joined us for dinner,' she at last begins.

I give her a store clerk's smile. 'Thanks. The food was great.'

The shower goes off. Celia looks with a start toward the bathroom. 'Look, I know you didn't want him here, but –'

'Celia, it's fine.'

She frowns. 'Really?'

'Yes. I mean, now that he's here, well, that's that, right?' This isn't what I meant to say at all. I had meant to say that I really don't mind, to be gracious and conciliatory. But the beers are operating and my face is hot.

'You don't sound okay with it,' she observes.

'Yeah, well, I don't really have a choice, do I?' She starts to protest but I cut her off. Celia may have scored by revealing the gaps in my sincerity. Fine. But I'll fucking well make her acknowledge the game. 'You've taken away my choice, right? You've made your judgment on the situation, and you've acted. Let's be honest here: you don't really give a shit whether or not I'm okay. You're more interested in teaching me a lesson.'

I take a swig of beer while Celia looks aghast.

'Proving your point,' I say.

'Which, for all I know, *needs* to be proved. I mean, it's probably a good thing not to let me have my way. I'm just being an asshole anyway?' Now I'm verging on tears and haven't a clue what I'm saying. What if what I think about myself is only that: what I think, not what I am. Then how do I know anything? Behind me through the kitchen, the click and whoosh of the bathroom door gently opening. 'I'm fucked up,' I say quietly. 'Don't pay any attention to me.'

Beer in hand I move quickly toward my room and shut the door. Tears are wetting my face now. Mystified, embarrassed, I slump on my bed, grab a pillow and wing it away. I do not have to be kind to everyone! I will not succumb to Celia's tepid world love, or Rash's pan-reverence. Ineffectual!

After a minute I lie back with my head against the wall. I can hear them murmuring. He probably heard everything from the can and now they're poring over it, bringing themselves closer. Although men aren't lining up for her, Celia's made a friend, it seems. Even when my sister was here, it was Celia who talked with her most. It must be acknowledged that I am the unsisterly one, and no one's busting down my door either.

Thankfully, there's no dreaded, inquisitive tapping at my door before I turn out the light. In the morning I linger in bed until I hear Celia leave, though it means being late for work.

Shirtless, Rash is reclining on his couch reading my newspaper. Cap gone, dreadlocks lying like twists of hemp about his shoulders.

'Hey, Rash,' I say as I rush by to the shower.

'Oh, hey, good morning, Hannah ...'

Under the refreshing cascade I calculate that if I skip breakfast, I'll have to see him only once more before I go. I dry my hair, wrap a towel around myself and stride hurriedly through the living room, flashing a thumbs-up grin. But Rash isn't fooled: he gazes up at me with compassionate eyes. On his chest, brown nipples soft in the morning sun.

The tears well up again as I'm stepping into my jeans and I work myself into a little fit hopping about, doing everything too fast, battling with my pants, my hair, and the irritating pang of desire for the flesh in the next room, those pools of eyes. Fucking men! They hang around your house half naked and think women don't notice, as if we respond only to *their* lust. Oh sure, flash your gently sloping belly – doesn't faze me. The Greeks didn't know shit because the male is of course above being provocative, floating in an ether of thought until he decides to whip out the goods and –

Check the mirror: confirmed, you look like shit, Hannah. To compensate, I put on a shapely crimson top I usually reserve for going out.

'See you, Rash,' I say, flying out the door.

His eyes register the top and his mouth opens, but I'm not sure if he says anything.

Twenty minutes late and no one's replenished the coffee in the staff kitchen and there's already a crowd in the reception area, my co-worker on the front desk glaring at me when I dash up still sweaty from the bike ride and grab my intake schedule. Shawn is slotted in first thing.

In the waiting room he's there in the corner, dressed in yesterday's denim jacket and jeans, sunlight reflecting off his hair. He follows me into one of our false-wall cubicles.

'How was your night here?' I ask.

He shrugs. Slouched in a chair across the round table, he looks even smaller. He flicks his head to shoo the bangs from his eyes, seems disinclined to speak. Fuzzy from hunger and lack of caffeine, I search for a conversation opener. 'Are you from Vancouver?'

'Up north.' Obviously that's all I'm going to get.

'So what can we help you with?'

He shifts. 'You said something about work.'

'That's right. What are you doing now? Are you on welfare?'

'No.' He looks at me softly. But as a lover or a mother?

I leave aside the question of income, since I'm pretty sure how he's living already. 'And I take it you're not in school,' I say. Shawn rolls his eyes, grins. I smile back, remembering how ridiculous classes seemed back then, how hopelessly out of touch.

I start formulating an action plan. I pretend, as always, that this is a science. Shawn qualifies for the province's youth programs, some of which are engaging and useful. I begin describing them, trying to get a sense of his interests. There's a terrific theatre program for street kids where they get room and board and can complete school credits while working on plays. I used to believe in this program. Today, my enthusiasm sounds forced.

Shawn examines his shoes. It seems the more professional I act, the more he recedes. Just killing time, perhaps.

'Tell me what kinds of things you enjoy doing,' I say.

He gives me a strange, wistful smile. His boldness with someone my age is amazing. The false walls lean closer, the atmosphere thickens.

Shawn brushes his hair aside without taking his eyes from me. 'How long have you worked here?'

'Five years.'

'Five years,' he repeats, and we stare at each other, me with an uncertain grin and him with a meaningful look that I can't decipher. I'm lightheaded, my brain a dry sponge. I look down at the form I should be completing, slotting him in somewhere, throwing services his way and hoping one of them takes him to a better place.

'You're really pretty,' Shawn says.

'Thanks.'

'Do you have a boyfriend?'

I laugh. No, no boyfriend. Shall we go hang out in an arcade?

'I'm an old woman to you,' I say. 'I think we need to get back to this stuff.' I indicate the form, but my voice is unconvincing. And I wore the crimson top, didn't I.

Shawn rises out of his chair and hunches over the table toward me as if to see the form better. Two kids studying, high school, those ignorant crushes blooming with such little effort.

I begin signing him up for the program I recommended. My pen moves slowly, my will entranced by the body so close to mine. Boundaries are essential in this work, we are forever told. These people need structure. Yet how can you discover a person's needs by holding back? Can help ever come from a closed heart?

I tell Shawn I'll make calls to see about some real housing until he gets into the program. He acquiesces to everything like so much triviality. He still needs a bed for tonight, so we go out front and I hand him over to my colleague. Shawn smiles and says he'll talk to me later.

The next hours are an increasing blur. At lunch I leave to get coffee and food for my raging headache. I wander up to Hastings Street west of Carrall, where the lower East Side suddenly morphs into a more prosperous downtown strip. At a tiny Lebanese restaurant I buy a falafel to go, then move on through the pedestrian stream. There are businessmen with defeated faces, women who walk with their eyes on the sidewalk. And some who look at me as we pass. Their eyes are as sensitive as nipples, and what do they see? Either more or less than what they are, a funhouse image. But it's only because I'm dehydrated and have an impossible job that I'm feeling frantic, that as I turn the corner my chest tightens in fear of what might come next: the sense that everything is so brittle, taped together and buckling. I can't go back on the front desk like this.

When I return I tell my colleague that I have to leave. I turn away from the anxious face, step uncertainly across the rowdy reception room and go out the glass doors. On the opposite sidewalk under an awning for a store long closed stands Shawn, waiting. He crosses the street toward the shelter, coming to claim me, and I can't move away.

The Road to Delphi

A car is climbing the mountain road. Sometimes it vanishes into the mountains or humped earth, surfacing minutes later. Sometimes it becomes a bright, travelling reflection of sun.

Oh God there's

The car. Alone on the road. Slowly.

Now. No

Yes I'm awake. 'I'm awake. It's not necessary.'

Poke. Prod. Fucking poser. Give her an ogle, it's what you came for.

'Ciao.'

That was almost funny.

So quiet. She's going

Hillsides in shadow. The car's headlights sharpening then. Closer.

A car is climbing the mountain road. The car doesn't appear on the road, it's just there every time, as if the road and the car climbing up it are inseparable. In the afternoon heat nothing but the car moves, a black marble rolling up and down the hills.

What time is it? I've lost my directions living in this room. Dozing. My sleep pattern's whacked. I can't get comfortable, can't relax. Must have been early morning when she brought the village doctor again, though I've said it's no use. A squat, hairy man with blackened nails and a farmyard reek. Prods my back, gets me to move my neck and arms, aims a pen flashlight into my eyes, mutters in Greek. Then exclaims, 'Good! Good!' I believe he's really a mechanic. As for the smell, they all raise animals here: even in Athens people kept chickens in tiny wired patios, a ratty goat munching table scraps. But the medic's main interest is Jude: follows her around the room, eyes fixed on ass. And the lady lacks a wedding ring. Here, that means something.

These dreams, flashbacks. The car, over and over. Hazy, toy-size, winding up the road with slow inevitability. Then I'm inside and sun-blind, with the bus swooping into view like a fallen planet and my hand spinning the wheel. Sound of glass shattering (clearly an embel-lishment, I recall only a thunk). My heart pounding out *you almost died*.

Up. *Up,* you. Table, wall, doorframe, railing, chair. God that's awful. Breathe. Okay? Now, carefully. Sit.

One can't complain about the view. These mountains, arid and worn as they are, remind me of home, especially Kelowna. Except here there's always the same hot high sun, the same shadows, and this eerie feeling of abstraction to it all, as if the world's been put behind glass, slightly shimmery.

Must be the heat and the pain. There's a horrible pinching grip on the back of my neck and my posture's crooked. The Tylenol 3s make me dopey. But at least I can totter out to the balcony now, a skinny Frankenstein with my bent and rigid walk, neck brace and cane. I've certainly repelled Jude. Seems like ages ago that she was hanging around exhausting me with her chatter, sulkily peeling tangerines. So determined not to visit the ruins until I'd recovered, though I said I'd be out for a week. And now it would be humiliating to complain – not after the endless, numbing disputes about my need for more solitude (in Jude's terms: emotional withdrawal, fear of intimacy, selfish-asshole syndrome …). She was late with my lunch today, sauntering in. At least it felt late. Perched on the table with her dress hiked high and described her day at the ruins: how she felt revisiting the ancient temple, what and who she saw, what and who she liked and disliked. Then off again 'for a coffee' with Erasmus, the 'fascinating' owner of the Hotel Apollo who speaks such excellent English, just as our guidebook said. Erasmus. What's that – Biblical? Not mentioned in the guidebook are his dissertation on Goethe and Schopenhauer, his five years in France and two published books of poetry. Claims to speak four languages. So why the hell is he *here?*

Such silence. Birds cut noiselessly between me and the moun-tains. Sometimes I think I hear singing or ringing, maybe church bells. I'll wobble forward, grip the balcony railing. Jude tells me hardly anyone's here. Apparently during the day the main street's walled with tourist buses, but people don't stay the night. It's hard to keep a business going. In this I hear echoes of untold hours with Erasmus, the pretentiously named poet down the hall with so much time on his hands.

I barely remember the last leg of the drive, our arrival at the hotel. My body propped against something, awareness constricted to the blaze of pain in my spine. But one thing cut through: a foreign face, regarding me. I see only the eyes now, unnaturally large and lighter than my own. Globes of Grecian blue.

The car on the mountain road. Brown and green slopes float up its windshield. Clouds.

Behind the glass, carefully driving, is a man in his mid-thirties. His face is still boyish but his hair's thinning, grown long and tied into a ponytail. His hope was that it would make him seem intriguing, but he just looks anxious.

I must be improving.

The recurrent memories and Rumpelstiltskin feeling are probably typical post-traumatic stuff, times a strange place, times pain. The last time I threw out my back I was down for ten days, and that didn't include a side order of whiplash. Nor the room without TV, air conditioning and telephone, not even a clock or memorabilia matches for the Hotel Apollo propped in a flirty Aphrodite ashtray. Erasmus is clearly a cheap bastard.

Today I caught myself dreamily picking up strands of Jude's hair from the sheets. Amazing how many there always are, how much she can afford to leave behind. She brought me dinner sometime after dark, then disappeared into the bathroom with a book that isn't ours. Came to bed once I turned the lights out. Is the sight of me that bad?

The trip began well enough.

Actually it didn't, but it showed signs of coming off, signs maybe only the deluded would interpret positively, but still. I'd imagined a romantic Atlantic crossing, a *bon voyage* to begin our second honeymoon, which is standing in for the first that never happened. Back then, something so contrived seemed uncool (and flat-out scary). Easier to slide from dating to cohabiting without fanfare, only years later – only now – sensing that some rites of passage might be necessary, a kind of architecture not built into our damp condo.

So the trip: a painfully organized year of planning and saving, my manly hard line against debt (like we've got any more debt to dig into). Political contortions, potentially fatal ones, at Learn English International to obtain an unheard-of month's vacation from Katrina. I'll be dodging bullets when I return unless her abuse of me as the school's 'favourite' (most exploitable) teacher and desire for me as the occasional, reluctant artistic mentor for her poetry can be carefully co-managed with some extra-long, agonizing coffee sessions on her 'voice'. Then the final week of teeth-grinding stress at home, the may-hem of departure coinciding with Jude's deadline for the *Journal of Hermeneutical Poetics* and the usual crisis: me acting as reader, editor, take-out fetcher, computer support-desk help and therapist (she still hasn't apologized for – or explained – calling me 'an obdurate fuck'). And in the end, when the yelling and whining and tears whittled us down to mean little nubs of hatred, acting as writer. So it always goes. The article has its moments. At least she manages to follow through with them, which is more than I ever did.

Two husks boarding the flight. Days on the noisy, cramped and pestilent plane before the chaotic change in Frankfurt, the airport a byway for every variety of disoriented humanoid, hard-wired Japanese professionals dashing to distant terminals alongside persons who looked like they'd walked out of the Red Sea. Culture shock in Athens: dismay at the dingy smog-covered hills, at the first one-star hotel where mopeds without mufflers orbited all night; at the crazed, tattered, mangy, emaciated, abused and ubiquitous Athenian alley cats (and later those goddamn kittens). But we seemed to be rallying the night we drank retsina and climbed Filopappos Hill to gaze at the spotlit Acropolis. (So far – despite my hopes for a miracle of fireworks – the only night we've made love on the trip: a weird, sweaty, semi-drunken congress in the dark with the mopeds roaring past the window and cats yowling in frenzies of fucking and hunger and rage. Jude twisted herself into the position again, making me hold her down with her arms pinned behind her back, as if only this way now – being entered blindly from behind – can she fully give in to desire.) In the morning the ferry to Santorini and a beach of black sand. Two days' grace. Then Jude gets her period, discovers she's forgotten her muscle relaxants because I pressured her to hurry up with the packing, and collapses on the floor of our room crying and grunting like an animal. My taxi ride to the village pharmacy, miserable with male guilt and the realization that romantic 'escapes' are great swindles: travel just forces your ineptitudes as a couple to the surface. But all was well again. On the overnight ferry to Chios we plied a sea like blue paint, our neat ripple trailing far behind. Jude let me give her a massage (though ignored what popped up). Sleepless in our tiny berth, I wandered into economy class before dawn and found gypsy children eating tomatoes, their dirty hands dripping seeds; bodies bedded down in the aisles, the bar jittery with red-eyed men drinking coffee, and curiously, a lone human stool left in the middle of the men's room floor. In all of this I felt a sweeping, symphonic beauty that was exquisite and indescribable, compared to which was the stubborn stone of my life. I leaned over the ship's railing to stare at the stars and wonder why we came. Mountains, islands, sea – like home, like the Canadian West Coast, but older. The mountains lower, the land long used and rough with archaeology. We yearn to get away from ourselves yet we choose the familiar, as if the distorted mirror holds the secret.

Was this what Jude and I had in mind for each other back in the beginning, when I was TA-ing for Poetry 100 and she was my cutest student, with an at-the-time endearing habit of comparing whatever poem we were studying to something that had happened to her that week? I must have been building up to Jude. She seemed an angel, and so she was – the purest incarnation, the avatar of my bizarre effect on women: the Editorial Attraction. For as long as I can remember, women have approached me not in lust, or even play, but with a 'Would you mind just taking a look at my _____?' (picture) (story) (lyrics) (essay) (film) (photos) (whatever). The confidant, the advisor. Yet no matter how gently and objectively it goes at first, the wheels of warfare or seduction (or both) start moving.

Two degrees and an exotic five years between us. Her smallness and fairness – I loved that right away. How I could grasp so much of her body so easily. Thinking that I'd never dated a younger woman and I'd always be ahead of her. Always.

Those were the days.

Clearly an invasion occurred when I wasn't looking. Someone else has been me for a while, and boy is he shitty at it. Futureless career, debt. An overpriced condo so damp that Jude is always cold. The phone jangles with calls from male friends, lesbian friends; people gravitate to Jude like moths. It's only a matter of time (isn't it?) before she leaves.

These thoughts are so familiar I can think them without thinking. They just go ping, ping, ping.

I used to write poetry myself. Where is that person? Maybe I thought I'd find him in Greece.

The car on the mountain road.

We'd been going up for hours. Windows down because there's no air conditioning in the cheap-deal rental I almost totalled navigating the Athens expressway. 'But it's a dry heat,' Jude kept saying, tying and retying her wind-loosened hair. She's been practically naked here, flitting about in short shorts and midriff-baring tops, exuding a gamey sexuality I haven't seen in years (and don't seem to be part of). Meanwhile my T-shirt was soaked, palms damp on the wheel. In the rearview mirror lay a thin blue line of cool, distant sea.

The road was relentless. It switchbacked, two narrow lanes wedged into the mountainsides without guardrail and barely room for one. Instead, those little shrines dotting the route. At first we paused to peer at some, fascinated by the stilted glass cases perched over the abyss and their tiny interiors of votive objects presided over by a saint's figure or picture of Jesus. Dried flowers, oil lamps, cups of holy water. Then one with a photo of a young man. Jude: 'Oh my

God, I thought this was just a pilgrimage thing.' I kept seeing his face as we climbed and climbed.

No villages along the way. The occasional road trickling down to some form of life. High up we found a gravel pull-over. Across the road on the slope, as if placed there by the Ministry of Tourism, stood some goats and a shepherd. They looked at us. Jude pointed and gasped. We got out and she waved, and the man raised a hand. He looked sunburned and tired. What kind of job for a man, a shepherd? Unmarried brother? Slightly retarded nephew?

We stood looking out at the view. Bells tinkled as the animals nibbled the tight tufts of scrub. 'I can't believe it,' Jude said. 'He's actually got a *crook*.' She kept turning her head.

'I thought that was made up. God, it's like seeing one of the seven dwarves. Do you think he really uses it on their necks?'

I remembered the kittens.

Jude wanted to go talk to him. We disagreed. She went anyway, sandals scrunching gravel.

When I turned around she'd climbed up and was trying out her phrasebook Greek. All blowing hair and white limbs, she seemed a pampered, pesky little pet sniffing the humbly clothed man, his woollen trousers belted with rope. The shepherd probably spoke a dialect. Probably this scene and like others happened all the time, busloads pointing cameras and recorders at the authentic Greek peasant – *with a crook!*

I went back to the view.

But when she returned to the car so elated, I was ashamed. Of course I'm jealous of her charm, her enthusiasm for people. For all my feelings of misunderstood alienation and uniqueness (too sensitive for the business world, too creative for academia), I'm just an insecure fool. Jerk, I thought. No wonder she wants to leave you.

We were almost here when it happened, when the afternoon sun appeared from behind a mountain and blinded me just as we rounded another death-trap bend. My sunglasses were useless; light seemed to envelop us. I threw up a hand and the car started veering. Jude shouted. I yanked the wheel. And then the bus shot into view, a sheared off chunk of Parnassos hurtling down with horn blaring.

Air shuddering the car. Jude screaming.

A swerve, a skid. Brake to the floor and lurching, my body still travelling at another speed, then caught across the ribs by the seat belt. A thunk. Glass breaking noiselessly. My neck snapped back and an arrow of pain in my spine.

I was slumped against the window. I think I passed out. Jude, unhurt but panting, was offering me cold water from the thermos, patting my face with wet hands. I shut my eyes. What did we hit? I heard her open the door, felt her on the seat minutes later.

'Look,' she whispered. I didn't want to. I imagined a lost goat on the road or worse – more death, like the knotted plastic bag of new-born kittens we found in an old orchard on Chios, tossed out like garbage.

I opened my eyes. Between her fingers, at the bottom of a chipped ceramic holder, lay a votive candle.

Early morning. An empty bed. A silent room.

Oh no, not like this.

I roll myself upright only to see Jude's suitcase, still on the floor.

Time to get a grip.

Grimacing, I stand and shuffle into the bathroom. As suspected the figure in the mirror is repulsive, with greasy hair barely hiding the scalp, blackheads dotting the nose, a mysterious scaly splotch in the whiskers. There's a roll of skin where the neck brace meets my jaw – a wrinkling effect that makes me look baggy, like an old doll losing its stuffing. With a lot of mess and a fresh dose of Tylenol 3s I manage to bathe myself and change. Then, for the first time in six days, I open the hotel room door.

An empty hallway. It's trembling, or I am. I should eat something.

I walk dreamily past identical doors until I find a small, mildly shabby reception area with a desk (a real desk, wooden, not the counter that we call a desk in Canada) on which sit a metal handbell, an unemptied ashtray, matches and cigarettes. A short, overstuffed bookshelf to one side. Tourism posters on the walls. I have no memory of this place, only those crystal balls of blue, staring.

Beside the desk, an opening hung with a beaded curtain obscures a living room laid out in what appears to be the typical domestic Greek style: plain and cramped. Looking around, I'm surprised. I haven't quite believed anything in Jude's reportage on the Hotel Apollo, the village, the mesmerizing hotelier. Despite the dreariness of our room I expected to find an alcove with erotic statuary, a languid hunk with his hand in a bowl of olives.

As I'm peering through the beads, a middle-aged couple knocks on the front door. 'Good morning,' says the woman, eyeing my neck brace and cane. 'Are zere any rooms right now?'

I invite them in with a smile, delighted to see other human beings after so long. There's a string of double keys on the hanger behind the desk.

The couple, who seem exhausted, confer briefly in front of a little placard listing rates, then request a double with a view and ask if they can check in immediately. They hand me their passports. I hand back a room key and wish them the best rest ever.

For a few minutes I examine the passports, then the bookshelf. There really are books in four languages. Many look hard fucking going, too. On the top shelf is a tome called *The Nude Through the Ages*. An inscription in French from Georgia, 1987.

I lay the passports in a drawer, light up a cigarette from the pack and step outside.

Was the street really this narrow? No buses. A rental car by the curb that isn't ours. No sign of ours. A man opens his storefront, the metal door rolling back with a clang. Here's the truth: there's no Erasmus here, and no Jude.

Maybe this really is the day of a new beginning. Maybe I was right about having to travel backwards to pick up the threads of myself. It's a strange country, a strange world: shepherds appear beside your car, village innkeepers read Schopenhauer. You think you know what history is but the airport's a tangle of timelines. Is it all a house of mirrors, minor distortions of sameness – when in Greece, your girlfriend makes off with your Greek counterpart?

I finish the cigarette, which picks me up like strong coffee. Ambling out of the village toward the ruins, I feel much improved. The morning air is fresh and warm, the mist in the valley soothing. My new life unfolds: Jude and Erasmus have gone, leaving me the hotel and the books. I'll stay in the village, devote myself to learning the language and maintaining the business. Develop routines: morning walks, afternoon coffee, olives and feta with beer under the stars. Read my way through the seasons. A loving family adopts me for the holidays. I take on a few students, bed some female travellers keen on holiday sex – but remain unattached. My first book, a poetic journal of lost love, is published to acclaim in Canada and wins the Governor General's Award. And then ... and then.

Where the road turns to descend the mountain, an ancient one made of stone goes up, winding through the deserted sanctuary. My limbs have loosened. Even my neck feels more flexible. I straighten up, hooking the cane on my shoulder, and start climbing.

The ruins sprawl up the mountainside. There's a blend of order and chaos, like a chessboard strewn with toppled pieces. I pass broken walls and rubble, fluted column rings, stelae, olive trees framed by old foundations. Everything is sunbaked and dry, the colour of light sand. In the centre of the ruins lies the temple of Apollo, where the Pythias, mere village women, surrendered to the divine and spoke his prophecies. The floor's still intact. Six massive columns rise above me, looking like chimneys, pipes.

As I continue the road becomes a path and the path ends high on the mountain above the sanctuary, at an ancient stadium. Stone bleachers that look only a little decayed, as if recently abandoned, climb up to a retaining wall bordered by thick, stumpy pines and tapered cypresses. I stroll onto the rectangular playing field then mount the cracked steps to the wall and turn around. The mountain falls into the far, faraway valley, past miniaturized trees to a misted blue-green plunge. Vertigo whirls through me and I grasp the wall. A breeze has come up, or I've just noticed it. Around the stadium, the plumes of cypress trees ripple and bend. My neck throbs, the hunger in my stomach is suddenly painful. I'm sweating – a lot. I look around at the trees, the field, the squiggled slant of steps. Everything is still yet seems to be trembling, the way electric lights and television screens shimmer when you look at them from the corner of your eye.

Something moves. It's a little cloud low over the slope, above the temple. Wispy as a puff of smoke, but with a denser, dark core. Smoke? It hangs suspended, slowly shifting its shape in the breeze but not losing any mass. The sky is clear. The cloud seems to have appeared from nowhere, from the rock itself.

I watch it for a while, still holding on to the wall. The breeze dies. Yet the cloud is still shifting, as if feeling the air around itself.

I want to get away. What possessed me to climb up here? Flimsy I am, hollow as scrapped metal rattling in the wind. My fingers creep down the wall, start to pull me along. I shuffle carefully, the sound of my shoes unbearable. The wall is so high, the ground under my feet a ledge inches wide. I can't take my eyes off the cloud. It's a menace, yes. An intrusion.

Get away from me.

My knuckles touch a second wall. An aisle descends into space. I press into the corner, shaking. I cannot get … where is Jude? I want Jude.

But you don't. No, you don't want her, do you. You want … nothing. Isn't that right? You won't love. Say it.

My knees bend. I slide rigid to the ground with a moan, and shut my eyes.

When I open them again, the cloud is gone. I don't even see it in the sky. Down below, the first bus of today's caravan is climbing up from the valley.

I return to the Hotel Apollo braced for anything – Jude gone, a recriminating old woman in black at the desk (Erasmus's mother), a note under my room door saying *Your wife. She call from Lesbos and say it better than you.* Most likely Jude with suitcase in hand, fired up for a dramatic farewell.

My back's hurting again. Besides being dehydrated, I have the blasted out feeling of returning from the dead (or near death), entering the Hotel Apollo for my second time the same way as the first. The other awful thing is that I feel terribly guilty, though that's often my state where Jude's concerned. In fact it's how I always feel in relationships, since I seem to evoke such frustration. Woman equals guilt.

She's waiting in the lobby to give me hell – demanding to know where *I've* been all day. Her hair's ratty from running her hands through it. There's a flood of memories attached to that gesture, to every inch of Jude, yet it bypasses me and I stand there not knowing what to do until I realize we're not alone.

Seated at the desk is a Greek whose large, almost incandescent blue eyes fix me quizzically. I remember the couple from this morning. It's an awkward moment. I deal with it by complaining of pain and heading to our room.

Jude follows. She seems scandalized that I'm feeling better.

I pick up a tangerine and start peeling. In few words, I explain where I was. Since she's still angry, I mention the missing rental car.

'So, we went down to the beach,' she says.

'What beach?'

She waves an impatient hand at the balcony. 'John, why didn't you leave a note? And why did you check that couple in?'

I see no beach. Far below to the west is a blue bay graded with lines of colour, seabed contours.

'What *were* you doing?' Her hand touches mine. 'Are you mad?'

I shrug.

'Can you please say something? You've been acting totally weird since we arrived.'

'I'm starving. I haven't eaten all day.'

Jude stares at me. Her hand caresses mine, but I don't respond. She's always touching me like a doll. It means nothing. Finally she says, 'Erasmus invited us for dinner. Both of us. He really wants to meet you, and since you're better, you can come.'

'Okay?'

We keep looking at each other. I recall a similar moment right before we left Kelowna to move to Vancouver. The balcony of our old place, the rooms inside stripped and packed into boxes. And in the great reduction of our lives, a frightening bareness. Each of us depleted and doubtful, regarding the other as if the antidote should come from them.

'Poor Jude,' I say.

She hugs me. I don't think she's understood.

Dinner is in a village restaurant on the Bay of Itea, which I saw from our room. Erasmus has brought a cousin named Stalios and they're both wearing golf shirts with jeans, which is a bit disappointing. I wish they'd be less neutral, less Canadian. I'm sweating in my shirt and long shorts, conscious of being the only man in the restaurant showing leg.

Jude sits across from me flanked by the two men, her face all soft and open when she looks at Erasmus. I don't know what to make of him. His lips are too full, almost lewdly sensual. He affects the pencil moustache of a Parisian intellectual, yet his curly hair is wild and coarse and dotted with lint. Everyone must be introduced to us: the restaurant's owner, tables of friends and neighbours. My neck brace is a big hit and compels Jude and me to tell the story of the accident, which we do, omitting our hit-and-run with the shrine. One small, elderly man kisses Jude with apparent joy and clasps my hand like I'm a long-lost friend, staring tearfully into my eyes and saying 'Canada!' I recoil, bewildered and moved that I've inspired such emotion. Erasmus says the man was in the war. Whether this is some historical reference I should know or a euphemism for insanity, I can't tell. Then we settle down and Erasmus tells us matter-of-factly, without bravado, to order whatever we want – we're his guests for dinner.

Stalios (same hair but not, thankfully, the eyes) begins telling me about the many scandals of the 2004 Olympics. 'Does this also happen in Canada?' he asks, as if ready to believe that there is a place somewhere without such inefficiency and corruption. I trade him stories about Vancouver's Olympic bid, and he nods, frowning, but concludes: 'These are not such bad problems. Your government gets things done.'

'John, come inside,' Erasmus says, rising and patting my shoulder. I follow him into the kitchen, which is hot as hell and rank with a dense, locker-room smell – goat cheese and fish, I suppose. Erasmus pokes into buckets and bins where fish lie quivering in murky water. He asks me which seem best, chooses four and calls over a cook. Then he wheels on me with a grin.

'So what do you think of our country?'

'It's beautiful,' I say, watching the cook.

He nods slowly, considering my cliché response seriously. I'm drawn to his eyes. 'Yes, it is,' he says with a sigh. 'You can get lost in it. The history, the old memories, it's like a dream. That's why I left for so long.'

'But returned.'

'The same reason. You can get lost elsewhere too.' He smiles. His eyes blaze like jewels. With the moustache he looks like a crackpot magician, a hypnotist, a fabricator of fortunes.

'Well, you must tell me about your home over dinner,' he says as we head back.

'Oh, I'm sure Jude's told you about it.'

'But that is not your perspective.'

'No.' I smile fatuously. 'No of course not.'

We eat *salata horiatiki, dolmades, skordalia,* black olives and grilled octopus, and drink two bottles of wine. More wine arrives with the plates of cooked fish, rosemary roasted potatoes and *tzatziki.* Jude, who can't hold her booze, is laughing too loudly, but the patio crowd is so noisy that no one notices. Her hair's spilling out of the bun she tied it in, falling in thick random strands.

'Stalios has been to Canada,' Erasmus tells us.

'Oh my God!' Jude's eyes go wide.

'He fell in love.'

'It's true,' Stalios says with a mournful smile. 'I followed her to Saskatchewan.'

'Not in winter, I hope.'

'Yes, in winter.'

I stare at him. Is nowhere disconnected?

Out in the dark a red buoy light blinks at the entrance to the bay. Everything flutters in the warm night wind: the plastic tablecloths secured with clamps, Jude's dress, jasmine and grapevine leaves on the trellis above. The wine is swirling into my Tylenol 3s. A chair blows over and gets dragged into the street. Jude laughs, her body twisted and her slim legs crossed high so one lovely bare foot dangles by Erasmus's knee, the ankle braceleted with silver, the toes polished a metallic blue. Erasmus leans toward her ear, and as she opens her mouth in delight, I catch her eye. There's a drunken gleam of comedy in it, as if she thinks we're both in on the joke. The spark brightens then falters, cools, and she looks away. I half wish I could be angry, or angry still – outraged that, rudderless on my own, I've lived as her ghostwriter, lived a ghost life, and she's let me.

Yet the glass is shattered, the anger gone like a puff of air. It's time to go.

The wind slides under my clothes. I see the four of us here, little figures under the twinkling lights. I see a figure rise from the table, say good night to Stalios, thank Erasmus and touch Jude on the cheek. Carefully, the figure gets into a car and drives away.

Two points of light swerve up the mountainside. The car emerges from the dark, parks, and the figure disappears into the Hotel Apollo.

The moon goes down in the sky. When the sun is risen and the mist lifted from the valley, the figure exits the hotel with a bag and cane. He begins walking toward the ruins.

As he approaches, he gets bigger and bigger. He spills out of the frame. You can see only his legs, and they're huge. What's he doing? He's muttering to himself, I think. Walking himself through, saying, Athens, three o'clock. Dinner. Movie. Bed. Ferry, seven a.m. The legs approach the first tourist bus of the day. An exchange with the driver. No, thank you, I prefer to wait on the bus.

For hours nothing happens. There's just the bus. A long, empty corridor with a window of valley at the end.

Then the tourists return from their late lunches. The engine rumbles, pumping diesel fumes through the floor. People fill up the seats, fill the bus with excited chatter. But you've been lucky: you've got the back seat all to yourself. The back seat is where the ride is wildest.

The Flying Woman

On Saturday at the YWCA, in my dance-fit class, I notice a woman who looks familiar. I think she's Claire Giroux. Forty-odd years have swelled and reddened her. Her prettiness is gone. Now, she just looks jolly. But as I watch her chatting with our teacher at the end of class – ingratiating herself, which was Claire's forte – I can see the young woman I used to know underneath, unchanged.

I pack and repack my bag until Claire has left (wearing a T-shirt and brightly striped pants that are wrong for her figure), and then I approach the table on which our teacher arranges scented candles and flowers as well as class flyers and, for my purposes, a box of alphabet-ized index cards for students to write down their contact information for receiving various notices. Fortunately, I've never filled one out. Now I do so, taking a moment to flip though the cards until one leaps out: Claire Giroux-Robertson, with a Kitsilano address below. How like Claire to create this inflated name!

Driving home through stop-and-go traffic, I feel enraged. Twenty non-refundable classes paid for just last week! I could switch my days to Tuesdays, but then I'd be back with my neighbour, Miriam Wentworth, whom I wanted to avoid, and I'd have to tell Miriam, a helpful but overeager person, that my Tuesday commitment has changed after all, which would seem strange. And I'd be stuck with her again, when my whole point in switching to Saturdays was pri-vacy.

It was smaller group today and in some ways surprising I didn't spot Claire sooner. It's embarrassing to think she might have seen me, watched me even. The dancing isn't exactly graceful. Part of the time we're just wandering the room on our own, 'pushing the energy' with our arms and legs like people trapped inside bubbles. And our teacher's always coaxing us to do pelvic thrusts and hip rolls, slinky movements that look absurd on older women. Miriam was correct about the therapeutic benefits though, because the class is very relaxing and already my back is improved.

When I arrive at Dan and Maria's, still very unsettled, Maria is dressed in her nursing uniform and braiding Malaya's hair. Though rushing off to work, Maria brews me a cup of coffee with cookies, which I gratefully accept. Efficiency and kindness: for all his career problems, my son knew what to look for in marriage. Their home, however, is in its usual chaotic state. I avert my eyes. Maria works twelve-hour shifts and cannot be blamed.

Raindrops are spattering the windshield by the time Malaya and I get to the beach, yet she's quickly out of the car and half-skips, half-runs ahead. I follow her to a point near the waterline and set up my chair. Malaya sits on her heels, already singing to herself, her small fingers raking the sand into mounds and ridges.

She'll stay that way as long as I let her.

I give her twenty minutes.

I don't want her dreaming any more than she does, becoming a moody, introverted misfit. Life brings challenges enough.

Maria has never talked much about the town that she and Malaya come from, a place called Infanta on the east coast of Luzon. 'A nothing place,' Maria once said. I think I can imagine: North Bay was a rough town too. And Lord knows what people thought of Maria having a baby and then leaving it behind when she went to Canada – they're Catholics, after all. Personally I admire her for getting an education, a profession. And Maria's mother clearly did a fine job with the girl.

'Malaya. Come here now, dear.'

She scrambles up immediately, even more obedient with Grandmother than Mother.

'Here's an apple.' I hand her a polished McIntosh, which she stares at.

'Do you know, Malaya, that this apple comes from a place not very far from here? People think of Canada as a cold country, but we can grow almost anything: pears, melons, berries, grapes. Not tropical fruits of course, no coconuts.'

Malaya grins. 'Mudder buy me coconut.'

'Yes I know. *Buy* them, of course! But I was talking about *growing*, right here. In farmers' fields.' Of course, there are fewer and fewer farms. When I ask for Fraser Valley potatoes at the supermarket, the kids think it's a brand name.

Malaya merely looks at me as if something is expected. Her nose is as flat as a baby's, barely emerged from her face. I tell her things and either they drop into her completely, regurgitated as answers to my questions, or else they pass right over, oil on water.

'Do you know too – go ahead and eat that, if you like – that British Columbia is a very, very big province? Some places are as hot as a desert, while others are as frozen as the North Pole. As the South Pole, too. Do you know your provinces yet?'

Malaya nods.

'Let's hear them then.'

'New found land. Prince Edward Island. And New ... there is other new.'

'*An*other. That would be New Brunswick. *Bruns*-wick.' I wait for the rest of the names to emerge, inwardly appalled at how mechanical the English language sounds when Malaya speaks. Her accent is unpleasantly nasal, her pronunciation primitive and grating. For flower she says 'flahra'. And I don't know how many times I've told her it's mo*th*er.

'That's very fine, Malaya.' I give her a pat on the arm (which I try to do often, though it feels unnatural), then get up and stroll down to the water, too fatigued for more talk. My concentration is scattered, thoughts squiggling off in all directions: Claire Giroux, my parents' apple trees, Dan as a boy. Burrard Inlet is busy with sailboats and motorboats, a few windsurfers; it looks like Lake Nipissing in summer. Yet how things change! The north shore, which was a forest when Nelson and I moved to Vancouver in the sixties, gets more urbanized each year. Chinatown keeps growing and growing, and almost everywhere I go now there's a bewildering blur of round, flat-nosed faces speaking languages I don't understand – including English. I can't say I like this. Who would? It took some adjustment when Dan brought home Maria, but Nelson and I did adjust. Now there's this imported Filipino child, a girl to whom one must explain the Great Lakes and the North Pole, and who doesn't ask enough questions; a child so quiet she materializes in rooms more like a scent than a person, a South-Sea flower far from home, like the little canoeing Indian in *Paddle to the Sea*.

Nelson, you missed all this. Sometimes I sit in our son's kitchen with his Asian family and don't know what on earth has happened. I can feel my mother and father looking through me, witnessing this wild tangent in our family line. It seems that, without trying, I've become very modern. At sixty-eight.

Saturday evening, when I'm finally back in my own home (apartment really, and there's another thing: the house that Nelson and I purchased now subdivided and, though legally mine, practically not. Below me my son, my tenant), I cook a hasty supper and try some pointless reading before opening a bottle of wine – something I've not done for myself since Nelson died. I don't want to be a withering widow, one of those supermarket ladies whose carts contain canned soup and pie. In old age Mother's diet devolved into pickles and chocolate, with a rye and water on the go from mid-afternoon to midnight. She also took to going around the house naked. The gas bill alone was obscene.

I sit on the couch waiting for the wine to breathe, and when I pour it, the smell is like magic. The first drink makes me feel as if I can fly to the moon.

The photographs are easy to find. All I have to do is pull out the shoebox labelled 'Infancy to 1963' from the storage closet. Inside are all the pictures from before my marriage, and among them one slim, faded manila envelope from my university years in Montreal. I carry it to the living room and refill my glass.

Photography is a strange art. Imprinting a moment on paper is supposed to be documentary, the camera eye neutral, and yet, looking at these pictures for the first time in decades, it's hard to believe they aren't illustrations of imaginary streets and make-believe figures. One in particular, of Michel and me standing outside our apartment on St

Hubert, strikes me as having a religious quality I don't remember noticing before. The portion of greystone house visible behind us could be from any century over the last millennium. Michel and I pose solemnly side by side, cloaked in long black winter coats like priestly figures, while flanking us are two icy mounds of snow with a polished, sculptural sheen. Most strikingly, Michel's frizzy red hair, which used to puff out hugely, is backlit and seems to surround his head like a saint's aureole.

That apartment was something! Half the third floor of a grand, early nineteenth-century house with moulded ceilings and wood strips gone soft with decay in the floors. Squirrels lived under the roof. There was a narrow pantry with deep, built-in bins for flour and grains. Heat blew from an oven with a wood-burning side converted to oil, so you roasted in the kitchen and shivered almost everywhere else. Michel's bedroom was at the opposite end of the apartment – Planet Pluto, he called it. And yet, I remember how it *did* feel grand: to be living in the centre of Canada (as it then was), and to come up the sidewalk under the ash trees and see the columned porch of our house, which had been built by a founding Québécois family. And to have Michel there. My parents never knew that it was Michel without the extra 'le', but I was in no danger of getting myself into trouble. We were just very good friends, really more like siblings. We'd met in first year and by second become very close; when his roommate moved away, it seemed natural for me to replace him. Michel and Theresa's place: balcony barbecues, Fish Fridays, friends dropping by, and cheap brandy nog in the winter.

I can find only one more photo of him. I never had any money in those days.

There are none of Claire.

The second Michel shot is more disturbing. Sitting in his favourite armchair, he's leaning forward so his face looms into the camera and his lips, slightly parted, emit a grey plume of smoke. Michel had a remarkable face. People always stared at him, though he wasn't handsome or even conventionally attractive. It was a cartoon-ish face, the features all exaggerated: wide mouth and long nose, gaunt cheeks, protruding eyes. Topped up with that crazy hair. In the photo, though, he looks tired, and his eyes have the lazy, distracted quality they sometimes got if he neglected his medication. He'd had a terrible family life and spent time in a psychiatric hospital at the end of high school. But in those days he was quite well.

It takes me a few minutes to notice something else in the photo: looped loosely around Michel's neck is a dark scarf, silk, I think, which slightly catches the light. Michel always dressed eccentrically and so the scarf could have been his. But I know in my heart that it's hers.

My sleep that night is terrible, practically non-existent. It's been more irregular since I sold the store, but this time I blame the wine. Near dawn I wake from a dream about Mother in which I'm cleaning her kitchen floor while she continues to drop coriander leaves as if I'm not there. I get up and dress. The state of the living room – couch cushions disarrayed where I initially fell asleep, the open packages of crackers and cheese, dirty glass and bottle I didn't remove – is unnerving.

I slip on a cardigan and head out to the yard, sending a passing skunk trundling for the hedge. A lovely mist enfolds the trees. The patio chairs have been left upright and Dan's little hibachi barbecue is out in the open and full of rainwater. I tilt the chairs against the table so they can dry, then clean out the hibachi and stow it under the tarp. It's still too dark for pruning, but I manage to get a dozen bulbs in.

As I kneel and dig in the cold soil, with the fresh night air clearing my head, I'm reminded again of the dangers of idleness. People are made to labour; a 'leisure society' only breeds crime and brooding self-destruction. It was idleness that got Mother medicated in her forties. True enough, all her people were unstable – grandfather gambled the family in and out of debt, grandmother claimed to see visions when menstruating, my uncle the surgeon was a Valium addict, and there were many obvious and sly drinkers. Father came from a better line and had his practice to concentrate on, but Mother, once we were grown, was empty-handed. Before marrying she'd done some painting. Lining our upstairs hallway were her canvases of the North Bay area, stormy lake scenes with shaggy pines and moon-silhouetted cliffs. When we children were young she often took to her room in midday, and if you pushed open the door she'd be lying there on her back, gazing at the breach of daylight between the drapes – or up, at the wooden mobile suspended above the collections of perfume bottles and votive figures on her dressing table. The mobile was a flying woman from Indonesia that Father bought for her during a trip they took to New York. The woman wore an ornate tunic painted green, red and gold like her feathery outspread wings, and on her head was a thin gold crown. Perhaps she was a goddess. Like a real bird she had no expression, though she did look intent as she swooped, her bare feet neatly pointed. I'd forgotten all about her until a few years ago when she started appearing all around Vancouver, in Thai and Indonesian restaurants, gift stores. As a child I'd thought of the flying lady as my mother's soul, the strangeness that gave her those moods and illnesses like no one else's, without coughs or vomit or other normal things that you could see and hear.

I dig in the last bulb under a pink sky. As I'm brushing the dirt from my slacks, Dan appears at the door in his pyjama bottoms. His chest looks very white. He's never grown much hair there.

'Mom?'

'I'm puttering. Couldn't sleep.'

I see him notice the chairs and barbecue with some resentment, but he says nothing, which is just as well. It's my yard.

The newspaper thunks against the front door as I'm having my coffee, but I can't get into it. My mind keeps going back to the dance class: I see the barefooted women rush across the floor, waving their arms and contorting their bodies, their fleshy bosoms and hips jiggling. Dancing among them with her loose, grey-blond hair is Claire Giroux, wearing a revealing black leotard and smiling.

Brandy. Cheap brandy. That was our drink back then, warmed with some milk. I cradle my coffee mug in my lap and remember: how Michel and I brought Claire back from the café where she'd charmed us, leading her along the snowy sidewalks of the Plateau, and how she huddled up to the stove and drank our spiked milk drink like a naughty cat. She was pretty and clean, an advertisement for shampoo. We gave her the living room to sleep in. She unpacked her rucksack and seemed set to stay as long as we allowed. What did we care? We were students. Claire didn't buy any groceries, but she kept her space tidy and we'd come home from school to find her cheerfully stirring a pot of *chai,* barefoot on the cold linoleum, her blond hair braided and tied off Indian-style with strings of beaded leather. And she was fascinating: the daughter of journalist parents, she'd been trucked across the globe much of her life. Cross-legged on the living room floor with a shawl around her shoulders, she'd tell us about cities with histories like old gnarled jungles. There were wonderful names: Ahmadabad, Djakarta, Rangoon. There were forests where giant stone heads lurked, deities that danced and laughed, and orgying couples carved onto temple walls. Monks interpreted dreams and doctors cured sadness with needles. Dawn came with a crash of squawks, gongs, cries, squeals and sizzling grills, but at night the breeze carried musical whispers. As I listened to Claire I felt lighter and lighter, as if only the mug in my hand prevented me from floating up to the ceiling like the children in *Peter Pan.* I would go to bed and lie there excited as a child, and the snow gusting against the window was like the spirits of all these animals and people calling me away.

She kissed me first.

I was so startled I just sat there on the floor with my drink beside my knee. I didn't raise my hands to push away or embrace.

I hadn't thought of Claire as beautiful, until then. Her mouth was small and tight. I could sense teeth, yet her lips were soft. She pulled back, smiling as she kneeled over me, and stared into my eyes like she could see right to the bottom. Her hands cupped my cheeks. I'd never seen a person so relaxed. Dear God, I thought, it's an angel. I felt drunk, though I'd drunk little. Afloat, though I could feel the rug's nap against my bottom. She kissed me again: this time her mouth parted mine, and I felt her hot tongue stroke my upper lip in a single, wafer-like touch.

She sat back and looked at me. Was I someone new, another being?

This all happened fast and slow.

Then she turned to Michel, who sat across from me wide-eyed, and she knelt and kissed him.

A flame leapt up inside me.

I saw Michel's lips move against Claire's. She seemed to kiss him longer.

Finally she pulled back as before, and on Michel was the same drugged expression that must have been on my face. His gaze lingered, unfocused and heavy-lidded, on Claire's lips. Then his eyes moved slowly over, to me.

What happened next I'd never experienced before, and haven't again. Perhaps it was because Michel had been so familiar to me. Known, I'd thought.

I felt something turning over end-on-end, coming apart. Michel uncrossed his legs and crawled toward me. He was transformed: in him was another presence, a regality I'd not seen or imagined. I reached up and he kissed me and I whimpered, then toppled over with his body wrapped around mine for I don't know how long, except then Claire was with us and we were all grasping at each other, licking and sucking like three ravenous infants, eventually naked skin to skin, on our backs, on our stomachs and knees, Claire's bare red bottom lifted to meet Michel's hips while she gnawed my toes and my tongue curled around his, a finger inside me, maybe mine, three rocking, moaning bodies twisted up into one, and then Michel was behind me, his thrusts burying my face in Claire's breasts.

Images from another reality, unimaginable even at the time. I remember a passing siren woke me to the dark apartment, which smelled of paraffin and sweat. I rolled over heavily on the cold floor: I felt like I'd fallen into rapids, been bashed about, and crawled out again half-senseless. My thighs were slimy.

I've had sex, I thought to myself. I've never gone past kissing and groping, and now this. What's happened to me?

Not just with a man, either. When it had been going on, I hadn't even thought about Claire being a woman. But there it was: lesbianism.

I lay staring at Michel's profile. He looked noble and calm, and I felt comforted. I got up stiffly and shook him.

'Come to bed,' I whispered, taking his hand. 'It's freezing.'

He lurched upright and followed.

'Claire's there,' he said, stopping.

'I'll bring her some blankets.'

'We shouldn't leave her.' He let go of my hand and went back, knelt down and said her name.

I went to get blankets. When I returned Michel was lying on the floor again. He spread the blankets out and closed his eyes. He's very sleepy, I told myself, so I pulled the comforter off my bed and lay beside him with one arm across his chest, my face against his side.

I could hear Claire breathing.

I never slept.

The next morning, Michel and I trudged to the bus stop like any other day except for the shocked silence. I was in a state; I felt desperate and hungry, crazed. Ordinary people passed us: they could have molested me right then and I wouldn't have cared. My body shivered like an exposed organ. Most of all I wanted to fling my arms around Michel and take him home to bed. But Claire was there. Instead, I asked him to meet me after classes.

Slender, black-coated, he was leaning casually against the university's entranceway off Sherbrooke Street, but up close I could see his unease. I kissed him on the mouth; he allowed it, but there was no desire returned. Then he grinned and made a poor joke that brought stinging tears to my eyes. We didn't touch again.

Not much time passed, maybe a few confusing days before the obvious became so: Michel had fallen in love. I came home one afternoon and saw Claire's rucksack in Planet Pluto, with her clothes piled on the floor. I left immediately and stayed out late at an all-night café, like some derelict, and when I returned and saw the two sets of boots and Michel's closed door, I curled up on my bed with a pillow mashed over my face. I'd been wrong all along: it wasn't Michel who needed our homey routines, but me who needed him. Now I was disconnected from everyone. I was corrupted, perverse, maybe a sex addict – and hopelessly in love. Surely I'd come to a terrible end on some muddy riverbank, or on a street like Duluth (where once we ran into a freakish character Michel had known on the ward). Why not? Madness ran in the family. I cried until I was dried out and making little hacking noises. Over and over I saw Michel's beautiful face, the one Claire had revealed, bending to kiss me. Why had she created these feelings only to thwart them?

The end of that term is a blur now. I recall that I ended up staying at a girlfriend's apartment, but I can't remember her name. I do remember, vividly, the day I returned to pick up my things, after exams were over, and found two men sleeping in my bed. Claire emerged from the bathroom wearing one of my sweaters and asked couldn't I wait until Dave and Ted, or whoever they were, had found a place to live? I wanted to grab those blond braids and throttle her.

'Dave and Ted? Where do you think I've been living for the last month? Who's been paying the rent? This is *my* room. This is *my* bed. We've been doing you a favour.'

Her eyes went all wide but I could tell she wasn't shocked at all. 'Well,' she said, 'you didn't have to just up and leave, you know. I think I also did *you* a favour. And I've done one for Michel, too.'

Such was her attitude.

Sometime the next year, a mutual friend told me that another man had moved into my room, and Claire with him. Apparently Michel was still living there and talking to himself in public. I hadn't seen him at school at all and had wondered if he'd quit. But I'd met Nelson when I was home that summer, and we were busy making plans for our future. What was the point of seeking out Michel? I felt sorry for him, but he'd become part of the past. It was embarrassing to have been so upset. Claire herself seemed to me a kind of exotic winter flu that had infected us.

And I got through it. That's the important thing to remember, I remind myself, sitting with my cold coffee at the kitchen table, though I feel flushed and exhausted from all this thinking.

The morning has begun; time to clear the cobwebs. I flick on CBC radio, tidy the living room, take out a roast to thaw for supper, and bake two dozen muffins for my son's family before noon.

Steady work and planning – that's the best medicine. When you have a purpose, things fall into proper perspective. Unfortunately, after Nelson's death in '96 I couldn't keep the store going on my own forever, and I'll have to find something more to do than babysitting Malaya and keeping house. But this past week has been very helpful. I've completely cleaned out and reorganized my storage, most of it old invoices and orders, financial statements going back decades, and now I know that all I must do is talk to my dance teacher about a refund, showing her the note I've obtained from my doctor stating that my back can't handle any unusual contortions.

Saturday morning I head out to class early. A cloudless and unusually hot September day, which is nice because Dan and Maria will be having a barbecue dinner. Entering the studio at the YWCA, my shoes echo in the unlit room. Usually our instructor's here by now, playing a CD of harp music or whale songs and arranging her candles 'to create a tone of openness and peace' among such bellicose women, I guess. I sit on a bench to wait. But she doesn't arrive. Other women come in and say hello. Someone turns on the lights. Every time the door creaks open I glance up anxiously, but now it's almost class time and the room is lively with chatter. I rise to leave. Just then, Claire arrives. She's dressed in a long black T-shirt and tights with Birkenstocks, and her hair's rolled up in a bun.

Claire Giroux! I still can't quite believe it.

Part of me has thought, this past week, that perhaps Claire never existed. That I dreamed everything, even that Victorian house. Claire is telling the women about a retreat she went on, being so charming. I keep myself turned away, but now here's the teacher swooping in with her CD player and an apology for being late. She's calling us into a circle to begin.

Leaving now will be conspicuous. Yet I'm not even wearing exercise clothes.

Quickly removing my fleece pullover, shoes and socks, I join in on the same side as Claire so as not to be seen. On goes some kind of African music, all tribal drums and shrieks. Holding hands we start stepping right-two-three-four, left-two-three-four, rush forward with a rising wail, patter back, then faster – right – left – rush in – cry – *Louder this time, ladies! Your voice needs to punch through the ceiling, needs to reach the sky!* – until I realize that my doctor's note will be useless if I keep this up. When the circle dance ends with much laughter I retrieve my bag and hurry to the washroom. Then I go upstairs up to the coffee shop to wait out the class. Ten past the hour, I head down and just miss running into them, Claire and the teacher, as they exit out to the parking garage.

Fine, I'll lose my money. It's just not worth the bother.

Nonetheless, back in my car I feel disappointed and a bit swindled. I feel like a royal fool. Once again, I've run away because of Claire Giroux.

Across the road, a rusted lime-green hatchback emerges from a parking lot and swings onto the street. It's Claire! I start my car and follow. I don't know why. I think I'm just irritated with myself. My hands and feet match Claire's turns, keeping in synch down to Pacific Boulevard, up across the Burrard Street Bridge, onto Cornwall Avenue and then up to 4th. We've passed Claire's street and possible shopping destinations, passed Jericho Beach and the turn-off to Spanish Banks, where I take Malaya. We're nearing the western tip of the city. Trees crowd up to the road. There's nothing ahead but the university, yet Claire ignores its entranceways and finally pulls over into a small lot on the western bluffs.

In my rearview mirror, Claire emerges and opens her trunk. By the time I double back I glimpse her disappearing into the woods with the bag she brought to class. I can't imagine what she's doing. Changing? Taking photographs? What *is* this woman? After all, didn't she blow into our lives only to blow them apart?

I enter the lot and wait for a while, but it's hot. When Claire doesn't return I get out and examine her car, which yields no information. Cautiously, I walk to the woods and discover a trail running down the steep hillface toward the ocean. The trees swish breezily. Sun spots sway and flicker on the ground. As I'm wondering what to do, another car enters the lot and a young couple gets out and heads past me. Once again I follow, though I cannot descend as nimbly on the rough path and am soon alone under the trees. But now I can see a brightness ahead, and a growing patch of blue. The sound of breakers reaches me.

When I emerge from the trees and step onto sand I'm not sure what's more bewildering: the sudden, exhilarating openness of the ocean from this point past the city; the unexpected crowd of sunbathers stretching down the clean, undeveloped beach; or the abrupt, up-close view of a naked man coming toward me.

A very *young* naked man, with muscles practically everywhere. He passes quite nonchalantly in his straw hat and sandals.

As I wander up the beach I realize where I've come, though I didn't know the way and had imagined an entrance much more guarded or grand. This is the place that visiting Japanese businessmen hire helicopters to fly over so they can snap pictures, so people say. But why is it called Wreck Beach? White sand, drift logs, green shield of trees ... the wreckage must have been historical. Or is it some other kind? Certainly no one seems worried about spies. People are lying about or standing in the surf, many of them naked as seals. I've never seen such an array of bodies, such varieties of shape. Parents, their breasts and genitals dangling, clutch toddlers or rub lotion over each other like primitives. There's an old man covered back and front in a pelt of grey hair. A topless woman waves a sign at me: Ten Minute Massage $10. Others are hawking sandwiches and bottles of beer. The sun is very strong on my head, and I'm thirsty. I wish I could ask for some ice. I turn around to go and standing right in front of me, in animated conversation with a man, is Claire Giroux – dressed only in her jewellery.

'Oh!' She turns and squints. 'Aren't you from the dance-fit class?'

My yes comes out more as a dying breath. I'm so ashamed, standing here like some voyeur.

'I thought so! Saw you there today.' She's smiling. Her breasts are huge and flat and drape over her a belly that's as rolled and puckered as bread dough. Below is a dark patch I strain not to notice.

'Didn't you leave early?' she asks, her brow furrowing. I'm obviously all wrong here, and it's not just the clothes.

'Yes. I … Claire, it's Theresa. Theresa … McDougall was my maiden name.'

A hand comes up to shade her eyes. I can see the name going round in her head, and then I say 'Montreal, 1962, the apartment on St Hubert?' and the name drops into place and her smile vanishes.

'Oh my God,' she says.

I wince. I wish Malaya were here with me, that I didn't look so alone, without even a handbag.

'I'm sorry for startling you,' I say.

'Theresa! I didn't recognize you, but now I do. My, look at you.' Claire shakes her head. Her eyes give me a very direct once-over, and then she nods conclusively. 'You look well! Are you, I hope?'

'Oh yes. Quite well.'

'Thank God. So many people I knew from those years are dead now.'

'Really?'

'Yup.' She nods and sucks in a breath. 'Cancer, car accidents … suicides, too. I look up old friends on the Internet and find their obituaries, scholarships in their name.'

'And what about, do you know anything about Michel?'

'Michel?' Her smile returns. 'Of course! Well, you know he became a sculptor, right?' (I nod, ashamed to admit I did not.) 'For a while he was having a lot of shows. I went to one at the Museé, but then I moved out here and lost track of him. You could probably look up his web site. Last I heard he lived on a houseboat or something, out east.'

She asks me about my life and tells me a little about hers. It's all too much at once, though. My thoughts are whirling; decades seem to have no form. All the things I've spent my life labouring for – my marriage, the business – have shrunk to minor bits of conversation now. Claire's breasts wag in front of me. I feel again like I did when I lay in bed after listening to her stories: that the world is fabulous and incomprehensible, with nothing certain to hold on to, and Claire herself like a genie popping in and out of my life to snatch the rug from under me. I've got to go, I say. One or both of us move forward, and

Claire's arms embrace me. My body goes rigid. She's so large! Surely I'll suffocate. But then one muscle surrenders, and another, and I sink into this warm blanket of flesh ... or am I rising? A tingling in my groin turns into a taut line reaching up through my middle and pulling. I'm getting lighter, floating. For a moment I think Claire Giroux is lifting me, bearing me up and away. I hold on to her shoulders as my heart soars.

After she departs down the beach with her friend Claire looks back and waves, and I watch and watch her. Then I turn toward home, where my granddaughter is waiting.

Acknowledgements

Some of these stories originally appeared, sometimes in different versions, in the following publications: 'The Road to Delphi' in *Best Canadian Stories 2004*, edited by Douglas Glover; 'In the Woods' in *The New Quarterly*, Winter 2006; 'Shelters' in *Prairie Fire*, Winter 2004; 'Remnants' in *Event*, Summer 2002. 'The Flying Woman' is available as an elegant chapbook from Biblioasis Press as part of their short fiction series. I'd like to thank the editors of these publications for their encouragement.

I'd also like to acknowledge the support of the Ontario Arts Council and the Canada Council for the Arts, and the Banff Centre for assistance with participation in the 2004 Writing Studio.

Sharon English's first book, a collection of linked stories called *Uncomfortably Numb,* was published in 2002 by the Porcupine's Quill. Born in London, Ontario, she spent six years in Vancouver and now lives in Toronto.